D0231679

THE WOUNDED HEART

There was no doubt in Lt Mike Gibson's mind that he was going to die. As a lieutenant in the Royal Army Medical Corps, death and carnage had been with him every day from the beaches of Normandy to the crossing of the Rhine. One moment eclipsed all others, in a forest clearing in Germany; where he had the experience of hell on earth. He owed his life to one woman, Lily de Howarth, the woman he adored. And now he was planning to kill her in the name of love . . .

Books by David Wiltshire
Published by The House of Ulverscroft:

THE TEARS OF AUTUMN

DAVID WILTSHIRE

THE WOUNDED HEART

Complete and Unabridged

ULVERSCROFT
Leicester

First published in Great Britain in 2011 by
Robert Hale Limited
London

First Large Print Edition
published 2012
by arrangement with
Robert Hale Limited
London

The moral right of the author has been asserted

British Library CIP Data

Wiltshire, David, *1935 –*
  The wounded heart.
  1. World War, *1935 – 1945*- -Campaigns- -Western
  Front- -Fiction. 2. Great Britain. Army. Royal Army
  Medical Corps- -Officers- -Fiction.
  3. Large type books.
  I. Title
  823.9'14–dc23

  ISBN 978–1–4448–1213–8

Published by
F. A. Thorpe (Publishing)
Anstey, Leicestershire

Set by Words & Graphics Ltd.
Anstey, Leicestershire
Printed and bound in Great Britain by
T. J. International Ltd., Padstow, Cornwall

This book is printed on acid-free paper

For Paul and Nettie,
Peter and Kate, Paul and Sue
— my family with love

Author's Note

In loving memory of Captain Maryse Croucher, QARANC, and for all those wonderful nurses who have, and are continuing to help, our heroes.

1

He left Harley Street in a cab called for him by the receptionist of Dr John Carstairs, with whom he had had a lengthy consultation.

Carstairs knew him very well, both as a professional colleague he had much admired as a student and because he had been looking after him for nearly eight years.

The good doctor had proposed surgery followed by a course of chemotherapy, but even then admitted he could guarantee nothing — not even a year. And he knew, from reading his own X-rays and scans, Carstairs was right. So today was his last visit — he had decided that.

As the cab lurched and rolled and swung its way through the congested streets towards his station, he finally made up his mind.

The thought had begun as he had sat before Carstairs' big nineteenth-century mahogany desk, listening as the surgeon had peered down through his half-moons at the notes before him, murmuring reassuring platitudes. As gently as possible, he had spelled out the seriousness of the condition he was facing.

The cab eventually pulled into the side of the station.

For his age, he walked well, only helped, when the arthritis was giving him a bad day, by a walking stick. He was now a sprightly seventy-nine year old.

Coming out onto the main concourse, he suddenly paused, arrested by an image from the past, brought on no doubt by the news he'd just received, news with which he was still coming to terms. Perhaps it was because he was standing where, as a very fit young man, he had crashed up the platform with his kitbag and brown suitcase, scurrying to board the train for his new unit — a draft of one.

He'd just finished his medical training, a shortened war-time course, and after a hurried six weeks of square bashing at the RAMC headquarters in Aldershot, he was joining a Brigade Medical Group, attached to some division or other, he couldn't remember the number.

The station was very different then, grimy, full of engines jetting steam up into the blackened soaring Victorian roof. Rays of sunshine had filtered down through the sulphurous smoke and evaporating steam to fall on coaches chock-a-block with troops, and on platforms with more columns of men in khaki uniforms with Lee Enfield rifles on

2

their shoulders, kitbags stacked in great piles, as they waited for their trains to be shunted in.

A shrill whistle rang out and the guard raised a big green flag.

His was about to depart.

Encumbered as he was, he ran as fast as he was able. Porters faced in the direction of the engine, raised arms and blew more whistles. The driver disappeared from his cab window, the locomotive gave a short blast on its whistle, and with a surge of steam on the rails before it, began to move.

He managed to get a door open, and then hands were reaching for his kitbag.

'I'll take that, sir.'

With it gone he swung easily up into the corridor, and drew the heavy door shut with a solid clunk.

Chest heaving, he turned. Everywhere there were troops standing or sitting on kitbags all the way up the corridor. A young fresh-faced corporal was holding his.

'I think the officers' coach is the next one, sir, just through there.'

He thanked him, returning the fellow's salute.

His carriage was also full, but at least the corridor was empty. After he'd clumped along its length, peering in the compartments at the men and women in uniform of all three British services, and Americans, mostly air corps, he resigned himself to sitting on his kitbag.

It took some time for the extra-long train to get up any sort of speed through the shabby, and in some places bombed-out ruins of North London.

He came back to the present day, shook his head as if to clear it and made his way down the platform, acrid blue diesel smoke drifting up from the power units of the train.

The first-class coach was halfway along its length. As he sank gratefully into his seat an attendant bustled down the centre aisle.

'Tea or coffee, sir?'

He asked for tea, and took an offered biscuit in its clear wrapping.

It wasn't long before the coach moved, almost imperceptibly, then diesel engines roaring, gathered speed. In minutes they were already slicing through those self-same suburbs, now at least brighter, but depressingly full of meaningless graffiti on any available space; walls, rail-side huts, bridges, even sides of houses. And beyond that there was endemic violence, drugs, broken homes. It didn't seem much like the Utopia they expected after the war, the one Lily had been so keen to help with its inception.

4

He closed his eyes to blot out the scene and woke up thirty minutes later as the train burst out of a tunnel onto the flat fields south of Bedford.

He watched the worked-out brickfields going past, the great quarries now grassing over, and water-filled, with flocks of seagulls fluttering on the surfaces.

As he watched, his mind went back again to that earlier train journey, recalling his mother's oft-remarked saying as she ushered him towards the stairs at the end of the day, 'Up the wooden hill to Bedfordshire.'

He started to doze again, still with the words repeating in his head.

Up the wooden hill to Bedfordshire.

Up the wooden hill to Bedfordshire.

The smooth whoosh of the train over the welded track gave way to the clickety-clack of the old, and the carriage rocked violently as they passed over points. The smoke of the engine drifted out across the fields, or billowed around the window through embankments. The telephone lines rhythmically rose and fell, rose and fell as they passed the posts lining the route.

They started to go by field upon field full of lines of parked new tanks — he recognized them as Churchills — with white stars painted on their turrets. The reality of the times and a grim reminder of what was to come, why the whole country was in a fever of expectancy: the Second Front.

Lieutenant Michael Gibson RAMC had qualified in 1943, followed by two short house jobs.

It was now March 1944.

★　★　★

When she first saw him she was in her nurses uniform, pegging her washing on the lines provided behind their barracks.

He'd just got out of a jeep, pulling his brown case after him as a corporal took his kitbag from the back seat.

He looked tired, slightly dishevelled, one battledress trouser leg starting to unravel above his gaiter.

In the brief interval, as he returned the salute of a passing soldier, he looked around wearily, blinking in the strong sunshine before he followed the soldier with his kitbag into the adjutant's office. But it was enough for her to fully see his face.

In that instance she had a feeling like she had never had before, so much so that she waited, still holding the wicker laundry basket to her hip, waited to catch another glimpse of him.

A nurse came by, paused.

'Are you all right?'

She frowned, didn't want to turn her head, but did, just for a second, and lied, 'Yes — just seen somebody I think I know.'

The other nurse said, 'What, the new doctor? He's due in today.'

She shook her head, replied offhandedly, 'Oh really? No, not him.'

She didn't add any more, just turned back and waited.

It looked as though her colleague was right. They knew a new doctor was due to be transferred in and he *was* wearing RAMC shoulder flashes.

It took ten minutes for him to reappear, walking with the corporal in the direction of the RAMC officers' quarters.

It was only a fleeting glance this time, but it was enough.

She decided to do something to make sure she met him away from the wards where Matron's beady eye was everywhere, but shook her head in disbelief at herself.

It was madness. What was it about a face that could do that, have that power? Certainly she'd never felt anything like it before.

That he might turn out to be a twerp, like so many men, was very possible, but she just had to find out.

She picked her way back to the cinder path that ran beside the nurses' quarters, and quickened her pace.

She was due on in fifteen minutes, but resolved, somehow, to find out his name before the end of the day.

2

A week later, and Lt Mike Gibson was wakened by his shared batman with a cup of scalding hot tea.

He shaved in the block with the rest of the male medical team — surgeons, physicians, anaesthetists, pathologists and dentists. For breakfast he dined in the mess on powdered scrambled egg and a piece of bacon, with a slice of grey-coloured bread.

Michael Gibson was clerking for a Colonel Gardham, a surgeon, and had other duties, teaching medical skills and hygiene to the many newly recruited rank and file of the corps.

This morning he had to give a talk to a section of the Queen Alexandra Imperial Military Nursing Service on recent developments, including the introduction of an apparently fantastic new drug called penicillin. He knew of it, but it was rare in civilian hospitals.

Fleming had recognized its anti-bacterial qualities at St Mary's, but a team headed by Florey had led the drive to produce it in commercial quantities. Ominously, it was now being stockpiled for service use.

Truth was, he wasn't looking forward to speaking to the nurses. He was really quite shy and, as a student, he had had his leg pulled unmercifully by them — when Matron wasn't around. What he didn't know was that they found his dark hair, brown, dreamy eyes and gentle manner irresistible.

But Mike Gibson was an only child from a working-class family, whose father had died when he was twelve. His mother had had to work all hours to keep food on the table, ending up in a munitions factory when the war started. He was conscious, even with a scholarship to the local grammar school, and then the medical school, that money was very tight — and that he owed it to her to make sure he qualified as soon as possible. So he'd never taken a girl out; in fact, since he was fourteen, he hadn't even kissed one — and even that was in a game of postman's knock, and he'd been hopelessly embarrassed.

As he came out of the mess and pulled on his cap he returned the salute of a passing sergeant.

He paused to breathe in the fresh air, and was joined by a colonel who looked up at the heavens and muttered — 'Hope to get a game of tennis this afternoon.'

They heard, before they saw, the steady

clip-clop of many feet, marching in perfect unison. Around the corner of the Nissan hut they came, a two deep column of twenty Queen Alexandra Nurses in their grey dresses with scarlet shoulder capes, and crisp, white head caps, arms swinging in exact harmony. It was purposeful, but strangely unmilitary, almost balletic in its rhythmic movement.

As they went past, their leader, a tall woman with the three pips of a captain on her red shoulders, called out, 'Eyes right.'

Immediately he was confronted by rows of soft faces as the tall woman threw up a smart salute.

He was deeply conscious of all the twinkling eyes and knew his face had gone as scarlet as their capes.

The colonel acknowledged the salute with the tip of his swagger stick to his cap then turned away.

The sister with the rank of captain responded with, 'Eyes front.'

But one girl stayed looking straight at him, blue eyes smiling mischievously. And then came an even bigger shock: she *winked* at him, and held him in her sight for a second more before turning her head forward to join the rest.

With swinging arms and hips the column proceeded into the distance, leaving Mike

11

Gibson feeling unnerved.

He thought the heat radiating from his face must be felt across the parade ground.

It wasn't lost on two corporals who were marching along in the other direction.

One said to the other out of the side of his mouth, before he threw up his own salute, 'They'll make mincemeat of that poor sod.'

Back in his hut he cleaned his teeth again, then got out the printed notes the army had prepared, and a few sheets of his own that he had written up — mainly headings in big capital letters so that when he lost his way, as he knew he would — he had no experience of public speaking whatsoever — he might be able to get back on track.

He placed them into his briefcase and made sure he had his fountain pen and the steel-rimmed spectacles that he had been issued with for close work, replacing his peacetime ones.

He set out for the lecture hut. From the main gate with its barrier and guardroom, the road ran straight through the centre of the camp, with regular branches off to the right and left.

On one side the huts were devoted to the sleeping accommodation and messes, the other to the wards, theatres and lecture areas of the base hospital.

As he found his way, stopping once to ask directions, he never stopped wondering at the size of the place. It was, he knew, designed to be a receiving hospital once the Second Front opened up.

He gathered it was one of a great many scattered all over the country, hinting ominously at what the authorities expected the casualty rate to be.

As he finally approached his destination, he realized the nurse standing stiffly outside the door, tapping one foot and glaring at her watch pinned to her starched white apron, was none other than the one who had led the column past earlier.

His heart sank as she drew herself up.

'Ah, there you are at last, Lieutenant.'

He noticed she didn't say 'Doctor'.

She held the door open.

'Please go in.'

He did, and nearly died. He was already on a raised platform, and before him were rows of chairs, and on those chairs were the nurses, chatting to each other.

As one they stopped and, with the scraping of chairs, stood up, staring at him. There was absolute silence until the captain said, 'Sit down please.'

She looked at him, rather contemptuously he thought, then back to them and continued, 'Lieutenant Gibson will be updating us on the latest drug developments and techniques being pioneered in hospitals and government research centres, for use both in the wards here and field hospitals overseas.

'Lieutenant Gibson.'

She stepped down and took up a seat in the front row.

Nervously he attempted a 'Good Morning, ladies', but only a croak came out.

He cleared his throat and tried again, this time with more success, but he was aware of twenty pairs of eyes on him.

His hands trembled as he opened his briefcase and took out his notes.

Nevertheless, he started quite well, he thought, even using the chalk on the board behind him without it breaking.

He was ten minutes into the lecture, and feeling pleased with himself, when it happened.

His eyes fell on her face, third row back and to the left.

She wasn't doing anything, no winking, no smiling, just a fixed innocent gaze that held him, like a snake before a mongoose.

It was as if all the others in the room had disappeared, that they were alone in a world without sound, without change.

But change did come.

'Lieutenant?'

The captain's icy voice broke into 'their' world.

Startled, knowing he was that God-awful red again, he tried to carry on. He failed miserably. Despite every attempt not to look that way, he was always drawn back to her.

Her face was the same, totally focused on him, earnest, serious . . .

Except — was it his imagination? — was one eyebrow now raised?

Was she laughing at him?

How he did it he didn't know, but he finally got to the end of the talk.

They all stood, chairs scraping again as he thanked them, then hurriedly stuffed his notes back into the briefcase, grabbed his cap and swagger stick and virtually fled the room.

Outside, he stepped out briskly, not caring where he was going, just wanting to get away from the disaster.

And the girl — what was he to make of her?

It was only when he realized his heart was thumping in his chest at the thought of her, that he began to realize just what an effect she was having on him.

Although he guessed he was probably on the end of a typical nurses' stunt — they were always up to no good as a relief from their demanding work — there was something about her, something about the way she looked at him . . .

And she was bloody attractive.

He wondered where he might next meet her.

Wondered what she would do.

Wondered what *he* might do.

3

The train began to slow. The attendant's voice over the PA brought him back to reality.

'Bedford next station.'

He stirred, opened his eyes. Outside, the outskirts were slowly going by, soon followed by the light engineering firms, a scrap-metal yard and finally the steel bridge over the River Ouse, with the town buildings beyond.

They passed the site of the old Victorian brick-built station, now a warehouse and car-park, and began to draw into the steel and glass structure that was the new station.

The crowd that got out of the train surged ahead of him, and were largely gone by the time he reached the barrier.

When he passed through he was met by the driver of the village taxi who had been booked to meet him.

'Good evening, sir. Did you have a nice day?'

He hadn't told him, or anybody, of the real reason for his trip to London, just said he'd been up to his club.

'Yes, thank you, Reg. Do you know if my wife has been all right?'

'No trouble at all, sir. According to Peggy she's been in the garden most of the time.'

Peggy was their daily help and wife of Reg.

He got in the car. As Reg hurried around to the driver's side he thought of the future, or lack of it for him, and what it would mean for his wife.

It continued to worry him deeply, brought him back to what he had been thinking of earlier. They moved off, Reg talking non-stop over his shoulder as the car eased out into the evening traffic on the main road.

Once clear of the town, to the relief of Michael Gibson, Reg stopped talking as a flurry of rain and oncoming traffic made him concentrate.

Michael gazed out at the familiar country-side where they had lived for over forty years, at least the bits of it that had not been covered by housing estates and bypasses and the like.

A lump came into his throat. It was the end of their life together that he was contemplat-ing, a life that had begun in another world, a world of horror, deprivation — and war. A world where Great Britain still had an Empire, albeit on the edge of disintegration, a world of service and sacrifice and, paradoxi-cally and because of their youth, the greatest, most momentous time of their lives.

18

* * *

After that first lecture, he kept a lookout for her, agonizing every morning as he shaved, with his braces around his hips, at the thought of what he would say, what he would do — no doubt make another ghastly fool of himself.

But she was nowhere to be seen, not on the wards, or at the lectures, or the labs — not *anywhere*.

Obviously she was intent on avoiding him. Desolate, he went about his duties, wondering how he could at least find out her name without arousing suspicion — and humiliation.

He did try a couple of 'Are you all present?' when confronted with the nurses at his following lectures, hoping they might call out names of those who were absent, but nothing ever came of it.

Eventually, when he was with a little group of them showing them how to use a latest piece of equipment, desperation got the better of him and he asked about the blonde nurse — the one who hadn't been around for a while — because he had some notes for her.

A mistake, he realized straightaway as they exchanged knowing glances and innocently

19

denied all knowledge of whom he could be talking.

In his agony, he didn't believe them for a moment. So when it happened, a week later, it took his breath away. He found a note in his pigeonhole.

Frowning, wondering who it was, the fine script in blue ink suggesting it wasn't official in any way, he ripped it open, aware as he did so, of a fresh lavender scent.

When he read it, his jaw dropped.

Dear Mike (may I?)

I've been away on compassionate leave because my dear grandfather died. He was something big once in the Foreign Office, so I have not been around for a while.

When I got back a couple of friends said they thought you'd been looking for me. I shall be in the hospital social club at 6.30 tonight if you still wish to meet.

Yours

Lily de Howarth

Shaken, he lowered the sweet-smelling fragment of paper. It was just not done for young girls to be so forward — at least not from his background. And she seemed so posh — that was unnerving.

But he knew he would go, in his best bib and tucker, or rather battledress.

He savoured her name, over and over. Lilian, Lilian de Howarth.

He reinserted the note into the envelope, conscious once again of the scent, and put it into his breast pocket, buttoning down the flap.

Tonight.

Six-thirty.

He looked at his watch. Five more hours. He wondered what would happen. To tell the truth she scared the daylights out of him even more now, with her boldness. What was he getting himself into? But despite his terror he knew he would be there.

Some unstoppable urge was driving him on.

4

The Honourable Lily de Howarth stood in her camiknickers before the mirror above the sink in the ablutions block of her hut. She was applying lipstick and powder — more than the authorities, in the shape of Major Brown, the Matron, would ever approve, but she could go to hell. Tonight she was on a mission.

Since she'd set eyes on him on that first day she'd been troubled in a way that had never happened before. She had turned her nose up at all the men she had grown up with — they were either too weak, or too bossy, expecting her to follow the pattern set out for a wife and mother, and to support them in *their* careers.

She had other ideas, and in any case, with the war, everything had changed. The young Lily de Howarth had seized the opportunity. As soon as she could she'd run away from finishing school and had worked in a factory before her father and mother had caught up with her.

But even they could not protest when she had applied and been accepted for training as a nurse, and subsequently they had been quite proud when she had enrolled in the Queen Alexandra Imperial Military Nursing Service.

Fine, for now, but 'Hon', the nickname she was usually called, knew that would only be for the duration of the war.

When it was over she would do something else, what precisely she did not know, but politics was becoming more and more interesting.

She pulled back from the mirror, pressing her lips together and then puckering them up. Satisfied, she put away the precious lipstick she had obtained from some Yanks in London.

But now there was this young doctor, Mike Gibson, to whom she'd taken a shine. With his looks, he certainly roused in her quite unusual thoughts — as her mother called them — but what was he really like?

Well, she would know in under the hour.

Back at her locker beside her bed she took out the one blue frock she'd brought with her. Raising her hands, she put her head through it, found the sleeves, and let it fall down around her. Buttoned up, and with the thin waist belt buckled, she turned from side to side, inspecting the result. Satisfied, she put her feet into her Cuban-heeled shoes, and did up the side-straps.

Lily found her shoulder bag, checked for her cigarette case and compact, then paused to take a deep breath. Right, time to find the truth about Lieutenant Michael Gibson.

Would he prove to be as good as he looked?

Mike got to the social club five minutes early, pushed open the door and stepped into the smoky atmosphere.

Disappointed, he couldn't see her anywhere.

A three-piece dance band, all in khaki battledress, was playing, and about fifty couples were moving steadily around the floor, the hanging mirrored ball turning slowly up in the ceiling, sending flashes of silver light onto the crowd.

He made his way to the bar, ordered a pint of the weak wartime beer, and was just giving a pound note to the grumbling barman who was saying 'Haven't you got anything smaller, sir?' when a voice, a soft, woman's voice huskily said, 'May I have a pink gin?'

He turned, found himself looking into big blue eyes, eyes framed by the falling locks of blonde hair gleaming in the dull light, never before seen in all its glory, usually pinned beneath her nurse's cap.

And lips as scarlet as the QA's cape.

He just stared.

She put her head quizzically to one side, eyes laughing. 'Is that a no?'

Michael Gibson jumped into action, turning back to the barman, who also couldn't take his eyes off her.

'And a pink gin, please.'

They said nothing until he took his change, then Lily picked up her tumbler and dipped it towards him.

'Thank you.'

He raised his tankard, and then took a gulp of his beer, wishing it was a short.

Lily sipped hers then murmured, 'So you came. I hope you weren't too shocked by my little message.'

He finally found his voice.

'No, well, yes, I mean — '

She laughed, a throaty chuckle.

'You don't know what to make of me, do you?'

Michael shook his head, grinned for the first time, a warm, sheepish smile that melted her heart.

'No, I've truly never met anybody like you.'

Lily, for once, was at a loss for words, and dropped her eyes to her drink.

Eventually she said, 'My parents tried their best, but I suppose I am a bit of a wilful nightmare. I'm sorry, I hope I haven't offended you.'

Michael shook his head. 'No, no, of course not.'

He stumbled over his words.

'I was flattered, after I got over the shock.'

She grinned. 'I promise you, even I don't make a habit of it.'

There was an awkward pause, then he said, 'Shall we sit over there?'

He nodded in the direction of a table in the corner.

She led the way. Following, he watched her slim figure, smelt the trace of perfume, and began to wonder where it would all end.

He was aware, too, of heads turning as she passed.

They sat down. Michael was glad to do so, because it was all like a dream, and he felt weak with the knowledge that the most beautiful girl he had set eyes on, was with him.

Wasn't she?

'So, how long have you been a doctor?'

He winced. 'Not long. Less than a year in total.' Embarrassed he added, 'Pretty green, really.'

Lily frowned. 'Don't be silly. We've all got to start somewhere. Did you always want to be one?'

He told her about going to the grammar school with no great expectations, of how it turned out he was good at natural sciences.

The biology master had suggested medicine as a career, something way beyond his wildest dreams, and how his mother had said his father would have been overcome with pride.

From that moment on he had worked day and night to make it come true.

Lily listened intently, eager to find out more about him. And she was aware, not that it mattered a tinker's cuss to her, that they were socially far apart.

He plucked up courage from somewhere to ask, 'And you, have you always wanted to be a nurse?'

She thought for a moment, running a finger around the rim of her glass.

'No. Got into it because I wanted to help — do my bit for the war effort — among other things. And it did appeal to me. My Aunt Florence was a VAD in the Great War.

'We have a wonderful oil painting of her in the library. In her eyes you can see all the suffering she must have seen — all the youth of her generation being mutilated and dying.'

She looked up, smiling to lighten the atmosphere.

'Sorry, getting quite poetic, wasn't I? Whether I stay on after it's all over, well, we shall have to see.'

Mike prompted. 'You mean, you'll get married, I suppose, and settle down?'

The look on her face told him he had said something that was controversial.

She frowned. 'Well now, whether I marry or not it won't be up to my husband to tell me what I can do, or can't.'

When she saw his stricken face she relented.

'I mean, I expect him to understand that I would need more from life than just to be his wife.' She looked up at him, from under heavy lids. 'You would, I'm sure.'

He couldn't believe he was hearing himself as he answered, 'But if there were children you would have to stay at home — surely?' he added lamely, realizing too late that she was looking unhappy as he spoke.

Lily raised a disapproving eyebrow.

'You sound like all the other men I've met. This is the 1940s, things are changing, have changed *already*.'

He nodded, frightened because he didn't want to rile her anymore.

Mike didn't know that she had already forgiven him, making allowances for his social background. The working-class male was as bad, worse in many ways, than the men from her background, but she considered that was not his fault — there was a

28

lack of education to consider, whether he was a doctor or not.

To fill the silence that might have developed, she added quickly, 'Anyway, after the war is over, there will be big changes in Britain.'

Relieved to be able to move on, he answered, 'You think so?'

Lily was quite definite. 'Nobody is going to go back to being just like it was before, are they? Remember the last time — after the war to end all wars, the land fit for heroes that never materialized!'

She remembered the passion with which her history teacher at Cheltenham Ladies, an ex-suffragette, had spoken, instilling in her the many radical ideas that were floating around in her head.

To be truthful, Mike Gibson had never thought about politics really, being far too occupied in clawing his way out of poverty by his chosen route.

He knew he had been considered a bit of a swot, but the thought of having to retake any of the exams filled him with acute anxiety. The scholarship was of limited value, and the consequences could have been catastrophic.

He shrugged. 'No, I suppose not.'

Lily decided that that was enough for now. She hadn't meant to carry on like this — her personal vendetta as her father jokingly called it. She rummaged in her bag, produced her packet of Benson and Hedges and offered him one.

He leant forward, took one of the long cigarettes he rarely if ever smoked, preferring the cheaper — because he could afford them — Woodbines, fishing out his lighter at the same time and holding it up as she put one between her bright red lips.

He spun the wheel a couple of times until the sparks ignited the wick, then watched as she sucked hard, the tip glowing red. He lit his own as she sat back, put her face up and let out a long stream of smoke through her nostrils.

She sighed. 'That's better. I needed it for my nerves.'

Puzzled, he pulled his chin into his chest. 'Nerves, how do you mean?'

Lily grinned. 'Meeting you, of course.'

Nobody, as far as he knew, had ever had 'nerves' meeting him before, quite the reverse in fact, and now this beautiful creature was saying just that.

'Me? That's hard to believe?'

She put her head quizzically to one side. 'Why?'

'Well . . . ' He was at a loss really, didn't want to say because nobody had before, or that she didn't strike him as the type to have 'nerves'.

Thankfully she didn't give him time to reply.

Lily grinned. 'I didn't know how you would react to my cheeky note. It was very forward of me, but how else was I to get to know what you are really like?'

He grunted, frightened to ask, but just had to. 'And now?'

She took another long draw on her cigarette, held it away from her, her other hand cupping her elbow for support, and took her time.

Lily's eyes were shining as she raised yet again one of those fabulous pencil-thin eyebrows like Carole Lombard the film star, and delivered her verdict.

'So far, so good. How about you?'

Mike Gibson's heart restarted.

He stammered. 'I . . . I — yes, very good.'

She furrowed her brow. 'Don't go mad now.'

There was a slight pause before he chuckled.

'Sorry, didn't mean to sound so uncertain.'

Lily giggled, and then they were both laughing. He felt more relaxed, and they talked for nearly an hour when another nurse passing by, said, 'Hon, don't forget you're on at nine.'

Lily looked at her watch.

'Oh my God, I've got to go.'

At the sight of his crestfallen face she explained, 'I've got to get this bloody make-up off — Sister will kill me if I go on the ward like this.'

He stood up to help her with her coat.

'Why did she call you Hon?'

She winced.

'Someone found out my father is' — she looked straight back at him, lifting her chin in anticipation of his reaction — 'Lord de Howarth, so you see, the Honourable — ' She shrugged her shoulders.

'Comes with the title. I don't use it, of course, well, not here.'

Mike swallowed, feeling even more out of his depth. As they walked towards the door and guessing he was feeling uncomfortable, she added, 'When I started my training at UCH in London there were several girls with silly titles, wasn't that amazing?'

He groaned. 'UCH you say. Couldn't be worse.'

She frowned. 'What do you mean, it's one of the best hospitals in the country. Where did you train then?'

With a sly grin he said, 'Kings — London.'

The two colleges and their hospitals were great rivals.

The rags between them were legendary, with the mascots frequently being kidnapped and subjected to indignities.

Lily gave a whoop.

'Oh no — I was once taken prisoner by your lot.'

She coloured at the memory. Lily and three other nurses had had to kiss the entire first fifteen before they'd been released. In fact, she'd gone out with one of them for a few months after that, even let him slide a hand up her thigh to the top of her stocking, and a bit beyond, before slapping it away — unsure of what would have happened if she'd let him continue.

He held the door for her as she went out into the cold night air. In the darkness he felt better, told her about his experiences.

'I went on a couple of rags to your place, before second MB that was, afterwards I was too busy really, except for one winter's morning when I was doing my obstetrics. I'd been up half the night delivering a baby — they named it after me', he added proudly, 'and had come back to the hospital when a crowd from your place came round the corner, pelted me with snowballs and took the damned department bike and my bag as well.'

'Oh my gosh.'

She held a hand over her mouth.

'Did you get it back — the bag, I mean?'

He nodded. 'And the bike, eventually. They took it apart and sent a bit back each week — by post.'

She giggled. 'I went a couple of times down to Kings.'

Without thinking he said, 'I didn't see you, I would have remembered.'

Lily stopped walking.

'You would have, would you?'

In the darkness his reddening face was hidden, but his voice was surprisingly firm as he replied, 'Yes, I would have.'

For a second she stayed where she was, then resumed walking slowly.

'Seems so frivolous now doesn't it, what with the blitz and everything, what were we thinking of?'

'A little light relief, letting off some steam. I wonder, when this madness ends, will it be so innocent again?'

She said, emphatically, 'Yes, I believe so. Anyway, we shall make it so. Come the first post-war general election, the people will show that they want change. Mark my words. I'm going to stand, you know. Daddy's got connections. I'll use them if I have to.'

His eyes widened.

'That will be as a Conservative, I take it?'

She snorted.

'No, silly, I'm going to be a Labour Party candidate.'

Shocked, his face, caught by the moonlight, must have shown it.

Lily chuckled. 'Surprised eh? Thought because Daddy's a lord I'd be a Tory?'

Bemused, he stuttered. 'Yes, well, or a Liberal.'

Lily cut him off with a sniff.

'Oh them. No, the future is Socialism. Cheer up. You're not the first to be taken aback.'

Mike Gibson, utterly captivated by this stunning creature, muttered, 'I see.'

But that was the last thing he did.

At the entrance to her block they stopped. She waited for a second or two for him to say something, but, as she was already late, she got on with it.

'Are we going to meet again?'

He was going to ask her out, it was just that he was struggling to get up the nerve, so he answered, 'If you like.'

Despairing, she said firmly, 'Yes. I like. So when?'

He just said it without thinking. 'Saturday?'

He had no idea if he was on duty or not — he'd get somebody to cover for him.

Briskly she nodded.

'Yes, I'm free in the evening. Can we go to the pictures?'

'Yes, of course.'

'Do you mind if we meet at that teashop near the cinema, at say five o'clock? You know how gossipy it can be around here if they see us leave together.'

He'd agree to anything, so he did.

With that she held out her hand.

'Thank you for the drink.'

He touched her for the first time as they shook just the once, then she was gone. As he walked back slowly he thought about the evening, and her.

One thing was for sure, he was smitten with Lily de Howarth, Hon or not.

Although he didn't know it, the Hon Lily, as she hurriedly pulled off her dress, took the risk of staying in her camiknicks as opposed to the issue white cotton knickers, splashed cold water onto her face and wiped off the make-up with a flannel, as she struggled into her nurse's uniform, was smitten just as much with Lieutenant Mike Gibson RAMC.

★　★　★

As the car turned off the main road down a lane, bringing him back to the present, he

36

thought how innocent, how inexperienced they were back then.

But what was to come, in only months, would alter that forever.

5

On the Saturday morning he had to make his surgical ward round. There were fifteen patients, mostly with broken limbs from assault courses, and broken jaws and gashed faces from the fights in the local town pubs.

As part of a deal he had struck, he then went to the medical ward to fill in for the man who had agreed to cover his evening.

He couldn't believe it. For the first time ever she was there — it had never happened before. As the captain sister joined him, Mike found Lily already standing by the patient's bed, looking gorgeous in her uniform. He couldn't stop himself looking at her, despite the fierce, searching glare of the sister.

But not once did Lily look him in the eye, which, despite the circumstances, he found crushingly disappointing.

When they had finished with the patient, he started to move on to the next one, led by Sister, leaving Lily to rearrange the bedclothes.

At the next bed he picked up the patient's notes and, as Sister spoke to the man who was lying on his face, he glanced back.

The timing was perfect.

Lily looked up from tucking in the patient, and did her wink.

Frightened to death he looked quickly at Sister, but she had her back turned and was bending down, still talking to the patient.

Flustered, but relieved, he struggled with the notes.

'Is anything wrong, Doctor?'

Sister's thick eyebrows had drawn closer together, and she was looking suspiciously from him to Lily, who was now innocently pouring a glass of water for her patient.

His hand flew to his forehead.

'No, no Sister, just a bit of a headache, that's all.'

She continued to glower until Lily disappeared into the sluice room with a pan.

He went off duty at 2 p.m. grabbed some food in the mess, then, in his room, unbuttoned his battledress, took off his boots, stretched out on his bed and lit a cigarette, blowing smoke rings up at the ceiling and wondering about that evening.

Lily de Howarth — he corrected himself — the *Hon* Lily de Howarth had entered his life like a whirlwind — no, if he was going to use a metaphor, a volcano, and an erupting one at that.

He hadn't thought about the war, and the

future, or his mother's recent illness, since they'd met.

His mother. What would she think if he brought 'Hon' home to their terraced house?

Then again, at this stage, that was wishful thinking. Perhaps she was just playing with him, would soon drop him when the novelty wore off. But she seemed sincere.

Was he making too much of it? He had no experience of girls.

Depressed at the thought, he swung his legs off the bed, went to the lavatory, flicking the cigarette butt into the pan as he pulled the chain.

Well, he decided to make the best of it; if his heart was broken, so be it.

Stripped to his waist he washed in cold water, then lathered up with his brush, and used his safety razor to shave.

He decided to dress in his sports jacket and flannels. The jacket had elbow patches, and had seen him through the years of medical school. His mother had bought it for him in a Burton's sale and, even then, had paid for it by instalments.

He found a shirt, and a fresh collar, and struggled with the stud. The last thing he did was to dab a little Brylcreem in the palms of his hands, rubbed them together, then passed them through his hair, finishing with his comb. With his raincoat over his arm, he checked his wallet, picked up his trilby, and took a last look around his room. He was walking down the corridor when he bumped into a chap called Jimmy who was covering for him. The latter looked him up and down and chortled, 'Civvies? If I didn't know you any better, I'd say you've got a date.'

Mike pulled a face and tried to pass, but Jimmy side-stepped to stop him.

'Come on, who is it? Is it one of our juicy little nurses with a starchy outer cover and a soft centre?'

Mike winced. 'For heavens sake, Jimmy.'

'Who is she then? Might as well let on — you know I'll find out in the end.'

In a hurry he gave up. 'Lily de Howarth.'

The effect on Jimmy couldn't have been stronger. His eyebrows shot up and his mouth dropped open. He even took a step backwards.

'*Lily de Howarth*? You're kidding?'

Mike paused.

'Why?'

'I've been trying to crack that little number for ages and you're telling me *you've* done it?'

Mike started to get annoyed.

'Why shouldn't I — you're not the only one who can ask a girl out?'

Jimmy roared. 'But *you*? Why should she

say yes to you and no to me?'

'Maybe because she trusts me to be a gentleman.'

Jimmy whooped again. 'Don't you believe it. They all pretend to be guarding their honour, but there's a war on, don't you know? Anyway, you can't tell me the Honourable Lily doesn't know her way around, get my meaning?'

Mike didn't know whether to hit him, or weep. In the event he just walked away.

He might have known it. It was all too good to be true. Depressed, miserable, he barely remembered to raise his hat as the sentry on the gate slammed his boots on the tarmac, brought his arm across his rifle and presented arms in salute. He joined the queue for the single decker bus. When it came, it was nearly full up. He pushed down the aisle as it jerked away through the gears.

★ ★ ★

Lily had a luxurious hot bath, more than the five-inch mark prescribed to save energy. She used one of her precious bars of pre-war soap to lather herself. When she'd finished, she dried her hands, found her cigarettes, then lit up and lay back in the hot water.

Somebody banged on the door. The

corridor was crowded with girls seeking to use one of the five bath cubicles — it was Saturday after all.

'Come on in there, hurry up.'

Lily drew in the smoke, savoured it, then lifted her chin clear of the water and blew it up at the ceiling. So, what would happen tonight? She couldn't find fault with Mike Gibson. Enjoying herself, Lily whispered aloud what she'd been thinking all day.

'Mrs Michael Gibson.

Dr and Mrs Michael Gibson. Dr and the *Honourable* Mrs Michael Gibson.'

Yes, she liked it. Of course, she would probably still use her maiden name, with all the weight it carried, for her planned public life.

Despite all the banging and shouting, and even the brief appearance of a face at the small window at the top of the partition, which disappeared with a crash followed by yells and laughter, Lily serenely carried on smoking and thinking. She was still coming to terms with the idea that he was the one. How could she be so sure so instantly?

She snorted. Sounded like one of those cheap sixpenny romances some of the girls read.

But she knew she could be happy with him. Apart from his looks, it was something to do with his honest, easy manner.

And he wasn't boring either, though he was painfully shy, which was endearing but —

She frowned.

Although she did not want in anyway an overbearing husband, she still didn't want a man who wouldn't be, well, a *man*. There were some things he would have to take the lead in —

Fumbling, she found a hairpin, pierced the remains of her fag, and took another pull on it, then lay back again. She knew a lot of girls weren't virgins any more. It was the war. Everything was changing. Young men wanted to love and be loved, for tomorrow they might cease to exist, and the girls were increasingly only too happy to oblige.

And that was before the Yanks came. Now there were the Piccadilly Commandos — hordes of prostitutes who did the most blatant sexual acts out in the streets and bombsites.

But for all her boldness, the one thing that worried her, no, being honest, frightened her a little bit, was too embarrassing to even talk about with other girls: the act itself.

Lily had a last draw on the cigarette, could feel the heat on her lips it was so close, then touched the end in the water where it died with a hiss, and made up her mind. She would give Michael a little help — to see if he really was the right one for her. It sent a shiver down her spine.

When the bathroom door opened eventually, Lily, clutching her cigarettes and her own bar of soap in her toilet bag swept past, pulling a face at the rest clawing to get in.

★ ★ ★

By the time he'd left the bus, joining the crowds on the pavement, the mist that had been hanging around all day had started to turn into a fine rain.

Dull lights from the shops glimmered on the wet pavements, and the ARP Wardens were going around ordering the blackout to begin even earlier than usual.

Mike found the Old Tea Shoppe, its door set between two bow windows. A bell tinkled as he pushed it open.

Inside it was busy, but there were people just getting up from a table in a corner. When they were gone he settled into a chair facing the door.

A waitress in a black uniform, with a white pinny and a small cap came over and began tidying the table top, brushing the crumbs into a little tray.

'What can I get you, sir?'

He explained he was waiting for someone, but ordered a pot of tea.

She bustled away.

He looked around. There were several uniforms present in the room, mostly army, with a couple of RAF and a navy type.

He felt uncomfortable, wishing he hadn't come out in civvies. In fact, he'd been lucky to be allowed to really, had asked permission, saying he was going to the local hospital to sit in on an operation and they didn't want him to be in uniform. Lot of tosh really, but he had wanted, for once, this special once, to be like it was before all this — he shook his head sadly — this war had started.

But then would he have ever met Lily? He chuckled to himself. Maybe — as a doctor in a mining district with her as the crusading MP.

Anxiously he kept his eyes on the door tensing at every figure that turned in, until the blackout blinds were drawn.

Then it was every time the bell tinkled and before he could see who was coming that he looked up, heart leaping.

Mike checked his watch. It was twenty minutes past the appointed time. The waitress kept glancing at him as she came past.

He began to worry seriously that he had been stood up, when the bell gave the tinkle, the door opened fully, and there she was.

Lily was wearing a cream-coloured rain-coat, with the collar turned up, pulled in tight at the waist with the belt tied casually, not buckled.

On her head was a small hat with a feather and a net that came down beguilingly to just cover her red lips.

He rose to meet her.

'Sorry I'm late, the bus was full up, had to hitch a lift, and who should come along but your CO.'

Mike looked askance so she added hurriedly, 'Don't worry, I said I was going to the pictures with the girls, but meeting my maiden aunt first, for tea, all right?'

'Oh.'

His look of relief made her chuckle.

'So — sorry I'm late, *Auntie*.'

Mike grinned ruefully, but the waitress appeared with her order book, and pencil on a string poised over the page.

After they'd ordered scones and more tea, she saw the clock on the wall.

'Oh dear, there's only three-quarters of an hour to the performance. I do hope we can get in, there's bound to be a queue.'

He'd forgotten what they were going to see — it was irrelevant to him, but he asked just the same.

She put her head on one side.

'Didn't I say? It's *The Man In Grey* — is that all right?'

He'd seen it already, but didn't blink an eye.

'Yes, of course. It's supposed to be good, isn't it?'

She began pulling off her gloves.

'A couple of the girls have seen it — came back raving about it.'

Mike wondered why the whole shop wasn't looking at her, she seemed so radiant. He couldn't take his eyes off her.

Suddenly she put out her hand, covered his on the table, said anxiously, 'Mike, are you all right?'

Thankful that she'd not said 'staring', he lied, 'Just tired.'

She sat back. 'Been working hard?'

'Called in the night. A three tonner came off the road.'

She frowned. 'I heard about that. I didn't realize you were involved.'

He nodded. 'One poor devil had multiple fractures. His jaw was in pieces and his tongue was split right down the middle — looked like a snake's.'

Lily grimaced. 'How awful. Is he OK?'

'We lost him — what a waste. And not a shot fired in anger yet.'

With the arrival of the scones they began to eat.

She noticed his table manners were excellent. It would have been awful if she'd had to say anything, but she would have — *later*. If Mike Gibson was going to be her husband, he had to be right in every way socially.

With the last of the scones, and a final sip of tea, she put her cup down.

'Right, we'd better get a move on.'

He leapt up, held the back of her chair.

Lily glanced up at him, pleased with his manners.

'Thank you.'

She brought down the net of her hat.

He pulled on his coat, and put his trilby back on.

She gave a chuckle.

Embarrassed, he asked, 'What's the matter?'

She nodded at the hat. 'Makes you look older.'

He winced. 'Is that a good or a bad thing?'

She laughed. 'Neither. Just an observation.'

He paid the bill, the ornate old till flagging up the little cards that said a shilling and fivepence halfpenny. She waited by the door until he finished, and then pulled it open and led the way outside. It was raining steadily.

'Oh dear, I haven't brought an umbrella.'

'Hang on.'

He began taking his raincoat off.

'What are you doing?'

Mike lifted it up, over her head.

'Here, use this to cover you.'

Lily took one edge.

'Only if you come under as well.' With that she snuggled up against him. 'Come on.'

As they walked through the wet streets, Mike was acutely aware of how close they were, could feel her hip moving as her heels clip-clopped on the pavement.

They turned a corner, to be confronted by a queue that snaked around the side of the Gaumont Cinema.

'Oh no.'

She stopped suddenly.

'You won't want to wait, will you?'

He moved forward. 'Of course — come on.'

They got to the back of the line, were there for ten minutes without any sign of movement.

The rain began to fall heavily. Shivering, he was just about to say that perhaps she would rather do something else, when the queue began to move forward. Rounding the corner the commissionaire came into view bringing his arm down to stop the inflow until the ticket kiosks were free again. They were nearly up to him when an usherette came out and spoke to him.

He turned and called out, 'Only singles left now — ten only.'

There were groans and people started moving away. His heart sank into his boots.

Desperately, he half turned under their raincoat cover, but she was already moving forward.

'Come on — it will do for a start. Some people from earlier shows sometimes leave halfway through a programme, depends on what time they went in.'

She waited while he bought two one and threes, the tickets emerging with a *clunk* from the polished metal desktop as he pushed his half-crown through the little opening.

Waiting, Lily shook his raincoat free of water. Together they went up stairs and through double doors into the darkness at the back of the dress circle.

An usherette moved forward and flicked her light onto the tickets.

'You know there are only singles left?'

Glumly he said, 'We do.'

'Follow me.'

She led them down the steep central staircase beneath the beams of light from the projector picked out by the rising smoke from hundreds of cigarettes.

On the big screen was the Pathé News showing a Liberty ship being launched sideways.

She flicked her torchlight at one seat halfway along the curved row, full of faces looking at the screen.

'That's one.' She turned. 'The other's over there.'

It was across the aisle, two seats in and easier to get at.

He motioned for Lily to go.

'I'll take the other one.'

She nodded, whispered, 'I'll look out for you in the interval.'

Seats creaked upwards as he went along, saying thank you to the people struggling with coats and bags. When he finally reached his place he sat down, glad to be out of the attention of the rows and rows of faces behind him.

What a fine evening this was turning out to be.

Morosely, he watched the news end, then the trailers for next week. There was a pause, then the B film started, a western.

Every now and then, he glanced across the curving circle to where she sat, her face caught in the flickering light of the projector. She seemed deeply interested in the film and never once looked across at him.

52

But she did, but never when he was looking.

When the film was over the house lights came on.

He stirred at the sound of seats turning up, but guessed people were only going to use the lavatories, or buy cigarettes.

Mike looked across and, to his horror, saw that her seat was *empty*.

He stood up, searching everywhere. Had she gone home?

'Michael, over here.'

He spun round. There she was behind him right at the top, in the back row, with a spare seat beside her.

Relieved, he began edging back out to the centre aisle, then climbed swiftly to where she was, apologizing yet again as he shuffled along the row until he reached her and sat down.

'How did you manage it?'

Lily chuckled.

'I saw a couple leaving and was up the stairs like a bat out of hell.'

He refolded his raincoat onto his lap.

'Well, at last, we made it.'

She squeezed his arm.

'We did, didn't we?'

She knew she was being forward again, but she sensed Mike Gibson was going to need all the encouragement that decorum allowed.

Further talk was interrupted as the lights dimmed, then with an audible click, the huge curtains began to slide back, the flickering light of the projector already showing on the still moving curtains.

Then the title came up.

THE MAN IN GREY

She leaned nearer to him. He could feel her warm breath, smell her scent as she whispered near his cheek, 'I do love Stewart Grainger, he's a real matineé idol, and James Mason's voice is so distinctive, sends a shiver down my spine.'

Somehow he felt very resentful of them both even as he murmured, 'Really?'

He didn't say he'd always found Phyllis Calvert and Margaret Lockwood very attractive in their different ways, which was why he'd seen the film in London last September.

Lily stared at the opening scenes, which she had seen with the girls when they had been training in London. True, she was quite happy to see the film again, because she'd only suggested it as a means of getting him sitting next to her in the *dark*.

Now, she was wondering would he do the natural thing?

She shifted in her seat nearer to him, and waited.

Ten minutes passed before she felt him move slightly. She guessed he'd put his arm across the back of her seat, but not touching her. With bated breath Lily waited.

Mike swallowed; worried she could hear him gulp. His hand was so near to her opposite shoulder — but he just couldn't bring himself to let it settle on her.

Frustrated, Lily contemplated what else she could do.

When out with other boys she had had to beat back their touching stroking hands the moment they had taken their seats. Warmth was one thing, taking her for a tart was quite another.

On impulse she turned her head to face him and found he was already looking at her. Their eyes met. They stayed like that for several seconds, and then she reached behind her, pulled his hand down onto her shoulder then turned back to the film, conscious of her bosom rising and falling with her increased breathing.

Mike was glad of the poor light — he could feel the heat in his face yet again. But he kept his hand there, albeit without any movement.

After a while, Lily felt his hand tighten on her and pull her nearer.

In the flickering light she smiled to herself — she recalled her father holding a newspaper over the fireplace to get the failing embers in the hearth going, and being gratified by the increasing glow behind the newsprint.

Surreptitiously she glanced around at him and wondered. Her father, not used to doing the work of their butler, now in the Far East fighting the Japs, had held the paper for far too long, and with a yell had had to drop it as the middle turned brown, then black, and finally burst into flames.

Would, she wondered, Mike be like that? The quiet, shy ones were often the worst, the girls all said. Would she regret leading him on? She didn't think so, but you could never tell.

The object of her thoughts felt his heart pounding as he contemplated his next move. Mike took a deep breath, and began to move his fingers gently on her shoulder.

Lily smiled, snuggled even closer, and put her hand onto his leg.

6

The car turned up the drive and came to a halt outside the front door, which was already opening.

A large woman dressed in a dutch apron, hair pulled back into a bun greeted him as he got out. It was Reg's wife.

'Did you have a nice day?'

'Yes, thank you.'

As she helped him off with his coat he glanced up the staircase.

'How has she been?'

'Very good. We went for a walk in the morning, just in the back fields, but it was very nice. After lunch she had a sleep, then did a bit of painting. She's had her tea and changed for bed, and now she's playing old records.'

Relieved that there had been no incidents, he said, 'I'll just go up and see her.'

'Of course. I've set out your supper on a tray in the kitchen in case you want to eat upstairs. It's cold meat and salad. Will that be all right?'

'Yes. Absolutely. Thank you.'

Mike hesitated at the bottom of the stairs

and looked upwards before putting his hand on the banister rail, and beginning the haul to the top.

Halfway he paused, not only to collect his breath, but because he wondered how she would be with him.

He reached the landing; the door to her room was ajar.

The sound of the trombones and saxophones of Glen Miller gave out their smooth rendering of 'Moonlight Serenade'. He stopped, remembering —

The hall was packed, a great mass of men and women in uniform shuffling around to the sound of the band playing the Glen Miller number.

It was their second time out together. At the end of their first date, on the bus back to the hospital, as they ostensibly talked about the film, he was already agonizing as to what he would do when they parted. Could he ever pluck up the courage to utter the words 'Can I see you again'?

The moment finally came after they had passed the guardhouse, not even hand in hand, and arrived at her block.

She stopped and turned to face him, saying, 'Thank you, Michael, I enjoyed the evening very much.'

It was like music to his ear.

He nodded. 'So did I.'

She smiled, said, 'Good.'

And waited.

Lily was sorely tempted to help him, but he really had to overcome his shyness. Anyway, if he looked as though he was going to flunk it, she would do the job in the end.

He shuffled his feet.

'When are you on duty next?'

Straightaway she answered. 'Six a.m. And you?'

Sheepishly, he said, 'Eight.'

There was a pause, and he knew it was now or never. Somehow he managed it.

'Can I see you again?'

Lily didn't answer straight away, though she wanted to.

Was it some deeply embedded feminine instinct — to use her courtship power perhaps the only time she would have such an advantage?

It was only a second or so and, as soon as the anxiety showed on his face, she answered, 'Yes, I'd like that.'

His relief was obvious. Mike blurted out, 'You would?' as though he couldn't believe it.

She chuckled.

'Yes, I would very much.'

Relieved, he said quickly, 'When?'

Lily had it already planned.

'Next Wednesday. There is a dance in the town hall.'

His spirits slumped.

'I don't dance very well.'

In fact, the last time he had done so was at school, in the sixth form, where they had been joined by the girls of the High School, as part of their preparation for their entry into 'polite society'.

The hospital nurses' dances and the medical ball had always found him at the bar, before going back to his lodgings to put in another few hours of study. But she brushed his concern aside.

'That's OK. I'll be ready about seven. Will you come here this time? I don't care if we're seen — do you?'

Mike just shook his head.

Elated, there was still one final moment to surmount: should he try to kiss her on this their first outing?

Lily was wondering if he would. She decided to give him as much help as possible, and moved slightly closer and, as a consequence, had to tilt up her face to look at him.

It caught the faint watery light of the moon now riding clear of the receding clouds.

Mike was acutely aware of her presence, of her lips — dark against the moon glow of her face. It just came over him, like a powerful magnetic force. His hand went around her waist and pulled her to him as his lips closed over hers.

They stayed like that for seconds before he had to draw breath.

Elated, he gave a wild grin.

'Goodnight, Lily.'

It was the first time he had used her name. With that he turned and walked away around the corner. Then he ran, punching the air.

Behind the closed door, Lily leaned back against it, smiled, and whispered, 'I think you'll do just fine, Michael Gibson.'

7

But her plans, and Mike's dreams, were crushed when they were all ordered to assemble to hear an address by the hospital commandant, accompanied by Matron.

They managed to exchange brief smiles as Lily passed by with all the other girls, to sit somewhere behind him.

When the CO came in they all stood up, but he waved them down again. He looked around, at the sea of young faces and wondered. Back in 1918, as a young lieutenant, he had seen so much death and suffering, and had lost many school-friends. What would be the experience of this generation? He dreaded to think.

The CO cleared his throat.

'By the start of the year, it must have been pretty clear to most of you that something big was in the offing, and now it doesn't take much to guess that there is going to be an invasion of Europe — sooner rather than later.'

There was a babble of voices. He held up his hand until it was quiet again.

'We are going to be a part of that moment

in history and, as such, our detailed training is about to begin.'

More voices. He let them talk for a moment or two. When they ceased he continued, 'We are going to be designated Number A418 General Hospital, British Liberation Army.'

He looked directly at the nurses.

'You are to discard your traditional grey and scarlet uniform and will be issued with battledress, complete with boots and gaiters, tin hat and beret. You will also wear khaki tunics with skirts when not in the field.'

At this the girls broke into excited chattering, until Matron bellowed, 'Silence.'

The CO grinned. 'However, ladies, there is another side of the coin.

'As from tomorrow, you will be sent away in batches to begin training with commando sergeants who have been assigned to put you through your paces, make you fit to join Monty's force. You will be going on cross-country runs as well as extra PT — and drill.'

There were some groans until Matron's steely eye silenced them.

The CO folded his arms.

'There will also be extra lectures to prepare you for working alongside male orderlies, and to instil in you all' — he looked around

— '*flexibility*. We shall need it where we are going.'

The words seem to hang ominously in the air. For the first time the hall was quiet.

The CO turned his attention to the officers and men of his command.

'Gentlemen, besides your duties at the field hospital, you will be trained to serve at short notice in regimental aid posts, field dressing stations and casualty clearing stations. As I said before, flexibility is the name of the game. The sort of things you will need to brush up on are the initial treatment of the kinds of injuries the battlefield inflicts, little tips like if a man has been shot through a main vein, and the limb is cold, don't waste time, cut it off. And a casualty with a fractured jaw — our dental colleagues will know about that — treat for shock, pick out any loose teeth and bits of bone, then put a stitch through the tongue and tie it to a button on his jacket before you send him down the line on a stretcher.'

He paused, looked around at them.

'That's the sort of thing you will be taught in the next couple of months — the knowledge of those who served through the last war.'

When they were dismissed, there was no

opportunity to speak to Lily, only to watch her as she came out of her row of seats. Briefly their eyes met. She looked serious.

That evening there was much talk in the mess of the CO's address, and a growing anticipation of the assault on Hitler's Fortress Europe.

'Bound to be thousands of casualties,' said somebody, setting his pint back on the bar, 'You mark my words — it will be a bloodbath — like Dieppe, only worse.'

Mike couldn't stand it any longer and abruptly got up and left.

On his bed he began to write a letter to his mother. She was alone in her little terraced house, still working all hours of the day and night. In peacetime he could have begun to make life easier for her, but not now. He did not mention Lily.

The latter was with the five other girls in her group, some in dressing-gowns, others standing in their knickers and petticoats, hair in curlers as they spent the last hour of the day before lights out, on themselves. The talk was all about the movement orders that had been posted up while they were at the assembly.

They were all going to Peebles, near Edinburgh, to be put through the fitness and flexibility course. And tomorrow, they were being issued with battledress blouses, trousers, berets, tin hats — the lot. As promised.

The excitement was terrific — tinged with not a little apprehension at the thought of what it was all in preparation for. Lily's own excitement was overshadowed by regret. She would be parted from Mike. Their coming date would be the last for a few weeks, until she got back from Scotland.

On the Wednesday he spruced himself up, standing before a cracked wall mirror slicking his dark hair with Brylcream. With a last whisk of the comb he straightened up, satisfied, as he ever would be.

'Christ, you should be in the bloody RAF,' came from a passing captain in his vest and underpants.

Mike's face creased with anxiety.

'You don't think I'm overdoing it do you?'

The man waved his hand.

'Don't mind me, I'm just browned off. All this talk of invasion has left me slightly unhinged.'

Mike frowned.

'We're not actually in the front line you know.'

'Front line? I was at Dunkirk. This war doesn't have a front line like the last time. Ever heard of aircraft, Panzers, that sort of thing? And it's not like the old days is it? The Nazis might not care about Red Crosses.'

The thought of Lily in danger suddenly came home to him, wouldn't leave him as he crossed the camp to her block and waited by the door.

A couple of girls came through the doors, eyed him up and gave a giggle as, arm in arm, they hurried on.

When she came, to his shock, she was in her new khaki uniform, a lieutenant's two pips on her shoulder, little brimmed cap on her head.

It brought the dread welling up into his chest.

The smile when she had seen him, drained from her face.

'What's the matter?'

He shook himself.

'Bit of a shock seeing you in uniform, that's all.'

She lifted her chin defiantly, but turned around before facing him again.

'The skirt's baggy, but what do you think?'

He didn't like seeing her in uniform, but he meant it when he said, 'Beautiful.'

She chuckled. 'Flatterer.'

They walked to the bus stop, past the sentry who came to attention and presented arms in salute.

Being the nearest, she brought her hand up to her cap peak.

Out of the corner of her mouth she muttered, 'I'm not very used to this.'

He smiled for the first time. 'Cheer up, neither am I.'

Outside the town hall, milling around were crowds of servicemen and girls. Military police, in the form of British Red Caps and American Snowdrops, as well as ordinary policemen stood around in expectant groups.

Her face fell. 'Oh my gosh, I didn't realize it was going to be so busy.'

As much as he would have liked to find something else to do, her disappointment spurred him on.

He took her elbow and guided her through the three-tonners, taxis and buses that were bringing more servicemen into town. When they finally got inside, crowds were dancing to 'Moonlight Serenade'. They looked at each other in dismay.

Lily sighed. 'Don't fancy that crush.'

Relieved, he said, 'How about a drink — upstairs?'

While he queued at the bar she went off to see if she could find a table on the balcony overlooking the dance floor.

When he was eventually served and pushed out of the crowd with his drinks, he looked around to see where she was.

There were tables all around the balustrade, all occupied.

When he did find her, it was to see her laughing and joking with three American airmen at a table. One of them was holding her hand, looking at something.

He'd never really felt jealous before, and it was soon swept aside by disappointment. Was Lily a flirt?

As he arrived at the table she looked up, saw him.

'Ah there you are. Guys, this is Mike, my fiancé.'

Immediately they were all over him, slapping his back and shaking his hand as soon as he set the drinks down.

'Good for you, Mike.'

'Congratulations.'

'Great stuff, bud, you must let us buy you Champagne. Hey Lou, do they sell Champagne here?'

'When did you propose, Loo-tenent?'

'What?'

Quickly she pushed her hand in front of his face, showing off a sparkling antique ring on her left hand, third finger.

His jaw dropped in amazement as she said, 'It was very romantic, wasn't it, Mike?'

She looked up at him, eyes shining.

'I was in the sluice room — that's where we empty the bedpans, when he came in and went down on one knee — '

They all roared with laughter, with more slapping of his back.

After several more minutes 'Lou' said, 'Well, guys, it's time we left these good folk alone.'

There was another round of handshakes and kissing of Lily.

When they'd gone, she said, 'Nice boys, a long way from home.'

He looked quizzically at her, said nothing.

Sheepishly she confessed, 'All right, there was no room anywhere. All I said was, we'd just got engaged, before you went overseas, and this was your last night. They gave up their table for us.'

Shocked as he was at her brazen dishonesty, all that went round and round in his head was the word — fiancé.

Eventually he pointed at the ring.

'Oh *that*. It was my grandmother's, Mike. I normally wear it on my other hand. You men don't notice anything but the wedding finger.'

He shook his head. 'I don't think I'll ever be able to trust you again.'

She chuckled. 'Who said you could in the first place?'

8

They spent the next ten minutes looking down at the mass of dancers moving around the hall beneath the huge glitter ball.

At one end, behind the band, were the flags of the United States and Great Britain. The air was thick with cigarette smoke. It was only then that he realized that the orchestra was that of the Allied Expeditionary Force conducted by Major Miller himself, his rimless glasses catching the light every time he looked up.

No wonder the place was heaving.

He took a sip from his pint glass.

'Those Yanks, did you see their medals?'

She had, but a lot of people had medals in wartime.

'Yes, why?'

He pursed his lips. 'They were Air Force Crosses and Purple Hearts.'

Puzzled, she asked, 'How do you know things like that?'

'I did a month on exchange to one of their airforce base hospitals, all part of the push to try and co-ordinate our systems. Anyway, tomorrow, the day after, whenever, they will be back flying daylight missions over Germany; they and our boys at night are the only ones taking the war to the fatherland and occupied Europe at present.'

Lily frowned. He seemed to be going serious on her.

'What's the matter, Mike?'

He fingered his glass, wondering on earth why he was suddenly talking to her like this. And why now? He'd had the concern for some time. But he knew really. It was the sudden development announced by the CO. He said, 'Don't know how I will behave if we ever come under fire.'

Lily snorted. 'You'll be just fine.'

She looked at him, and something came over her that she had never experienced before. She wanted to reach out and take him in her arms, and comfort him. Not like a nurse: more like a *wife*.

Frightened by her feelings she stood up.

'Come on, let's dance.'

He looked at her, still feeling dejected, and protested, 'But somebody will take our seats.'

Lily pointed to where she was standing.

'We'll dance here.'

She grabbed his hand and began to haul him to his feet.

Mike put his right hand around her waist

as she put her hand on his shoulder and smiled up at him.

'There, is that better?'

He nodded. 'Sorry.'

Lily began to shuffle, nothing like the steps he'd learnt at school. He began to shift his weight from one leg to the other, and got closer.

Others on the balcony started to do the same, but he was unaware, lost in the sensation of being so close to Lily, her slim body pressing into his.

It was a slow number, a soft voiced singer asking *Why do robins sing in December?*

She laid her cheek against his chest, her sweet-smelling hair right in his face.

After a while her hands joined behind his neck, and in response he put both of his around her waist.

They stayed like that, even as the singer ended with *I know why and so do you* and the orchestra signed off with a flourish.

Suddenly she turned her head, upturned face just beneath his.

It happened so naturally, so gently. Their lips touched, and they stayed, sharing each other's breath, each other's warmth.

Eventually, somebody brushed past, jolting them from their trance.

Reluctantly they parted, sat down without

a word. Lily took a sip from her glass and peered at him over the rim and said quietly, 'You know I told you I'm going off to Scotland tomorrow.'

Miserably he nodded.

She laid the glass back on the table, contemplated it for a moment, and then said quietly, 'Will you write to me?'

Mike wanted to be sure. 'Would you like that?'

Lily nodded. 'Very much so.'

They both knew it was serious. If you were writing to someone it implied more, far more, than just a casual affair.

And, at that moment, Lily began to think very seriously about what she had thought of in the night. Then, it had been sometime in the future. Now, it was what she might do sooner — even tonight.

She shivered slightly at the thought.

The war had had its effect on her as much as on him.

The riotous dancing below brought them both out of themselves. They watched as with the stomping of hundreds of feet, the band stopped playing, and several hundred voices shouted in unison 'Pennsylvania-Six-Five-oh oh oh.' Then the orchestra came back in.

As soon as that number finished they went straight into an even faster tune, the dancers jumping around, hanging onto each other by one hand, the girls sometimes turning under it like some wild highland dance, at other times being pushed away, spinning like tops, to be stopped by the outstretched hand of their partners, their skirts flying out and showing their stocking tops, then snapping shut with each change of direction.

'Oh look.' She pointed. 'There are our Yanks.'

He followed her direction.

The Americans had their jackets off, were leaping around with three good-looking girls.

Lou suddenly threw one of the group over his shoulder. As soon as she landed he pulled her back through his open legs and swung her up in the air, legs pointing at the ceiling.

Lily effected an American accent.

'He sure can jitterbug.'

They watched until it came to an end.

'Would you like another drink?' he asked.

She turned to face him.

'Really — I'd like to go now.'

Not unhappy, he asked, 'Are you sure?'

She nodded. 'Yes. It's been fun, but it's too crowded.'

As they edged their way out, a voice boomed over the speakers, 'Ladies and Gentlemen, take your partners for a Paul Jones.'

There was a hub-bub on the floor as the girls organized themselves into a circle facing outwards, all holding hands, as the men did the same facing inwards.

Mike thanked his lucky stars. The thought of being amongst that lot, of having to face whatever girl was opposite when the music stopped, and dance with her, filled him with horror.

Outside, despite the blackout, the moonlit street was full of drifting servicemen and crowds of screaming women, staggering between pubs, all lit by hand torches and the dimmed headlights of the trucks and buses.

Military police and bobbies were still present.

Suddenly there were shouts, and the sound of smashing glass up a side street.

Several police from each group made in the direction of the trouble, drawing truncheons and nightsticks.

He grimaced. 'I don't think it's a good idea to wait around for a bus, do you?'

She threaded her arm through his.

'Let's walk. It's a fine night.'

'Are you sure, it's a couple of miles?'

Lily sniffed. 'How many miles do you think a nurse clocks up on the wards each day? Besides, I'm off on this course tomorrow — it might help me.'

There was the sound of more glass smashing and men running. That settled it. They began to walk rapidly away, but not before a passing bunch of Yanks wolf-whistled and called out to her, 'Hi, sweetie. We've got nylons.'

Mike found his free hand bunching into a fist, but Lily just laughed, and called back good naturedly, 'You know what they say —

Over paid

Over sexed and

Over here.

Goodnight, boys.'

Still hooting and whistling they went merrily on their way.

She was aware of Mike's tenseness, and said gently, 'They are only behaving like that because of the war.'

He knew she was right.

It grew quieter as they walked out past the gasworks, with its smell of coal gas.

At the railway crossing the gates barred their way. Eventually the dark shape of an engine came out of the night, the light from the fire box only partly screened off from enemy aircraft by the tarpaulin rigged between the footplate and tender. The ground shook as it clanked past in a cloud of swirling smoke and hiss of steam, flat wagon after flat wagon went by with the dim outline of a tank on each one. It seemed ages before the guard's-van hissed past, its dim red lamp on the back disappearing slowly into the distance.

Somewhere a signal crashed up, and they could hear the signalman in his box operating the big levers. The gates began to open.

As they crossed the track a cheery 'Goodnight' came from out of the darkness above them.

They called back in unison, 'Goodnight.'

Once past the last few houses, and out onto the road at the crest of a rise, the great expense of the starlit sky, with the moon riding like a queen of the heavens, made them pause, arms around each other.

Lily breathed, 'Isn't that marvellous? Ever since the blackout I've been fascinated by the night sky. It's never been so clear, so bright before.'

Mike looked from the stars to her upturned face.

He gave her a squeeze.

Lily squeezed back and sighed. 'I'm sorry I've got to go tomorrow.'

He grunted, 'I wish you weren't.'

Lily looked again at the stars, then leaned her head against his shoulder. She felt so comfortable, so safe, so *happy* with Mike. It was if she had known him for years — for ever. It was going to be terrible being apart, even if it was only for a month or so. Lily knew then, in that moment, that she was going to do it, that she wanted it to be *him*, and *now*. She took a deep breath. 'Would you like to come to the staff room in the day block — for a cup of coffee, just the two of us? I've got a key?'

In his excitement he wondered, did it mean anything more than just a nice way to end the evening? Then he worried about her.

'I don't want to get you into trouble.'

Lily snorted. 'What are they going to do — court martial me?'

After they had turned in past the guardroom, and were well out of sight Lily grabbed his hand.

'Come on.'

She led him across grass, then into the dark shadow between deserted wooden huts.

He tripped on something.

'Bugger — sorry.'

He'd lost contact with her but Lily's voice came out of the blackness close by.

'Stay there. I'll get the door open, and turn on the gas ring — it will give enough light for you to see the door. I can't risk turning on the main light even for a second.'

Obediently he waited, heard a key being touched several times to a wooden door before she exclaimed, 'Got it.' He heard it turn in the lock, and the creak of the door as she opened it.

'Nearly there.'

After a moment a match flared, and with a plop a gas ring came on. In its bluish light he saw the entrance and slipped in, closing the door.

Lily was checking the window shutters. In the eerie light he saw a couple of battered leather chairs, and a sofa.

'Never been here before.'

She chuckled.

'We don't let the doctors know about everything — this is one of our bolt holes.'

Lily busied herself filling a kettle with water then getting a couple of mugs off their hooks before opening a cupboard and taking down a bottle of Camp Coffee essence.

He lowered himself into one of the chairs, and stretched out his legs.

'This is all very domesticated.'

Lily flinched.

It suddenly felt hot in the little room, and she began to undo the buttons of her tunic.

As soon as the whistle on the kettle started a low singing, Lily took the whistle off, leaving the kettle still on the ring, explaining, 'There's a sentry around, don't want him to hear it.'

After another minute the water really started to boil, splashing out of the open lip, the blue gas flame glowing orange. With a dishcloth she took the kettle off and poured the boiling water onto the mugs, then put the kettle back onto the hob, not on the blazing ring.

'We'll leave the gas on — so that we can see.'

Mike watched as she stirred the mixture with a teaspoon, then picked up a milk bottle and gave the top a sniff.

'Milk is all right. How much?'

'A good dollop, please.'

Still stirring, she poured it in. 'Sugar?'

Since it was rationed he said, 'Two spoons. Can you spare it?'

She half turned. 'Since I don't take it you can have my share.'

She came over and held out the mug. He took it, then quickly turned it round to find the handle.

'Ouch, it's hot.'

'Men — '

She sat down on the sofa.

In the weak blue light he could just make her out, untying and slipping off her shoes, then tucking her legs up beneath her.

He took a sip of the hot liquid.

'What time do you go?'

Lily didn't want to think about it, but it brought the urgency of the moment to the fore.

'Ten o'clock. To the station. Catching the 10.50 to London.'

He nodded. 'Right.'

Lily drank some of her coffee, lowered the mug, and held it in both hands on her lap.

He couldn't sense it in the dark, but her breathing had become ragged, chest rising and falling as she contemplated her next move.

'Mike . . . '

He waited, then when she didn't say anything more he prompted, 'Yes?'

She finally got the words out. 'We haven't known each other long, I know, but do you think — do you think it's possible — ?'

Mike just blurted out, 'I love you.'

Lily wasn't sure she had heard properly, and said with unintentional sharpness, 'What?'

Frightened he'd made a fool of himself, he swallowed, steeled himself, terrified of being ridiculed as he repeated softly, 'I love you.'

Lily just stared at him.

In the silence that followed, all she was aware of was her heart pounding so loudly she was sure he must hear it.

Praying that he couldn't see she was

trembling, she set her mug aside, swung her legs to the floor, frightened they would give way and came slowly across and knelt before him.

'Mike . . . '

She couldn't go on, but Mike Gibson knew what she meant.

He took a deep breath. 'Lily, I've never — '

She shot out her hand, and put her fingers over his lips.

'Neither have I.'

They searched each other's faces in the dim blue light, then he reached out, gently cupped her face, and brought her to his lips.

Any doubts Lily had had about his shyness, his assertiveness, soon evaporated as nature took over.

When finally she guided him into her, and she cried out in pain and joy, Lily was at last released from the nagging worry that she had carried with her all her adult life.

Afterwards they lay in each other's arms, overcome by what had happened. Eventually she smiled up at him.

'You'll have to marry me now, Doctor.'

Mike kissed her forehead, whispered in her ear, 'Yes, Nurse.'

They stayed together, content to feel the warmth of their entwined bodies, to gently explore each other until, near dawn, they made love once more.

Lily finally stirred as the faint light under the door turned brighter.

'I've got to go. Matron will play merry hell if I'm reported out all night.'

They stood up and dressed.

By the cooker she asked, 'Ready?'

He nodded.

She turned off the gas, and carefully opened the door. The eastern sky was just showing the first rays of the rising sun.

She reached up, and gave him a chaste kiss on the cheek.

'Goodbye, darling. I adore you. I'll write as soon as I get there.'

As she began to move away he held onto her retreating hand, kissed it before releasing her.

'Lily de Howarth, I love you.'

He watched her until she reached the corner of the hut, looked carefully around, turned, waved — and was gone. And some part of him went with her.

9

When *Moonlight Serenade* came to an end he pushed open the door, and entered. She was sitting in an easy chair, back to him, only her hair showing: it was snowy white.

★   ★   ★

Lily looked out of the carriage window, watching the smoke from the engine up ahead, drifting away across the fields to dissolve in the dark wet tree-line.

It had been a hellish journey, now in its twelfth hour. In London they had boarded a filthy dirty train at King's Cross for Edinburgh.

It had been grossly overcrowded, packed with troops going back to Catterick Camp, airmen returning to their airfields all over the east of England; and sailors, heading up to Scapa Flow. All the corridors were jammed with men and kitbags.

Fortunately the nurses had been given reserved compartments, but it was a struggle to get to the lavatory at the end of the carriage, and they had to run the gauntlet of all the men standing there — good-natured, but still very tiring.

And there was so much of the journey left to go. They had waited outside York for over an hour, with no explanation.

She wondered what Mike was doing just then. With closed eyes she remembered last night for the hundredth time. Had it really happened? Lily was so happy she was beginning to worry that she had imagined the whole thing. At that she smiled at her reflection in the window.

No, it had happened all right, her body told her so.

She felt warm and content with herself like never before. It was as if finding him had made her complete.

Mike was her kindred spirit.

Tired, she drifted off to sleep.

'Hey, wake up, sleeping beauty.'

A hand was on her shoulder, shaking her gently.

'We're here — at last.'

Dazed, Lily looked around. The carriage was lit in a weird blue light and the blackout blinds were down.

She joined everybody standing up, getting their brown cases from the overhead racks.

With a jolt that sent them all flying they

came to a halt in the gloom of Waverley Station.

Somebody said, 'Welcome to Edinburgh.'

But it wasn't their final destination. That was a hotel in Peebles. Any ideas of a nice comfortable room were dashed, however, when they jumped down from the three-tonners that had brought them from the station.

They were directed to Nissen huts that had been built on top of the hotel's tennis courts and lawn.

Groaning, they entered the freezing-cold huts and sorted out their beds. Beside each one was a tin trunk. Lily opened the lid of hers, and inspected the equipment inside. There was a valise, a folding canvas washstand, canvas bed, bucket, and even a folding canvas bath — all packed neatly into the tin trunk.

A stern looking nursing captain with a clipboard who had been checking their names, nodded at the contents.

'The good news is that there is a washroom for your ablutions; the bad news — you will be required to use them on exercises.'

'That's a bloody relief.'

The captain frowned at the girl who had spoken.

'Bear in mind that when we are across the

channel you will have to use them, like it or not. Now, tomorrow: Sergeant Forster of the commandos will be putting you through your paces starting at 0630 hours. Reveille is at 0600 hours. Dress — PT kit. Breakfast at 0730 hours.

'On this course you will have cross-country runs, swimming in the excellent outdoor pool, and some lectures on warfare and survival.'

The captain smiled. 'But we don't have a matron to bother us.'

There was a cheer. The iron discipline of their matrons was legendary.

By the time she had got herself sorted out, been to the ablutions block, washed, cleaned her teeth and changed for the night, she felt tired. She got out her writing pad and envelopes.

Settled in bed she began to write.

Darling Mike
Well, I've arrived after a hell of a journey. I miss you so much already.

My dearest sweet one, I don't want to be away from you ever again.

She paused, closed her eyes to rest them as she thought of what to say next. A minute later, one of the girls coming back into the hut nudged her companion.

'Look at Hon.'

Lily, head to one side was fast asleep, pen still in her hand, and pad on her chest. As they watched, the pen slipped from her fingers.

★ ★ ★

Mike came out of the ward, walked disconsolately back to the mess. There were no stars, just unseen clouds making everything very dark.

Lily had been gone for nearly two weeks now and there hadn't been a single letter from her. He'd heard there were problems with the post, but it didn't make him feel any better.

He made his way to the mess, checked his pigeonhole for a letter yet again. Although the mail drop had been that morning, he lived in hope that the disruption might lead to a late delivery.

It was empty.

He was observed by two grinning dental officers.

One called out, 'Looking again, Mike? She must be someone special.'

He knew that word must have got about that he'd been out with Lily — probably been seen in town. Now he was the gentle butt of jokes and hints because of his previous shyness.

He ordered a pint of beer, and sat in a battered leather chair, with the day's well-read and creased copy of the *Daily Mirror*.

The awful struggle for Monte Casino was finally over. The Germans had put up a ferocious resistance; it had been going on for months. It didn't augur well for the future.

That night, he slept badly and awoke with a headache. It wasn't made better by a still empty pigeonhole. No letter from her. Later he went to the dispensary and swallowed a couple of aspirin given to him by Sergeant Mack. It was one of those quirks of military life, but pharmacists were not allowed to be officers — something that riled him deeply as Mack was better educated than he was.

He gave back the beaker of water he'd used to take them with.

'Thanks — with what we've got on today I needed them.'

An inspection had been ordered, which commenced at 0900 hours. The hospital was tasked to be prepared for mass casualty reception.

All theatres were manned; all wards prepared and staff standing ready; all motor transport on full alert. Senior officers then toured the hospital. By midday it was all over.

Somebody said it must mean that it was getting nearer the day the balloon went up.

A week later he was returning from the mess empty-handed yet again, with no letter from Lily. By now he was beginning to feel desperate. He didn't want to make a fool of himself, and get into trouble with her when she came back, but he was seriously thinking of going to Matron — to see if he could get her address.

All sorts of things were going around in his mind, the worst that she had had some sort of accident. With the blackout they received a steady stream into his surgical ward with the sort of heavy armoured stuff on the roads, especially at night.

But she would have to be very seriously injured or — the unthinkable — *dead* not to be able to get word to him.

Mike made his mind up. He would seek an appointment with Matron. It was a daunting thought, but he couldn't go on like this.

His thoughts were interrupted by a corporal marching up to him and saluting. Frowning, he saluted back as the man barked, 'The adjutant presents his compliments, *sah*, and can you see him ASAP, *sah*.'

The first thing that shot into his mind was that his worst fear had come true, that something terrible had happened to Lily.

Then with a rush of guilt he realized it couldn't be her, they didn't know about them, and in any case there could be no official reasons for contacting him.

It must be his mother.

He took off at the run, leaving the corporal to spin round and look after him, scratching his forehead.

'Officers, they're all off their fuckin' rockers.'

Mike crashed into the adjutant's outer office, the latter's duty clerk rocketing to attention.

Mike looked at the adjutant's door.

'I've been sent for — Lieutenant Gibson. Is he in?'

'Yes, sir.'

The man moved to the door, and rapped once. A muffled voice called, 'Enter.'

The clerk opened the door.

'Lieutenant Gibson for you, sir.'

'Good, show him in, Corporal.'

Mike brushed past the man, stood in front of a desk and did a perfunctory salute at the captain, a non-medical man with a thin military moustache. He was in his late forties, and had medals from the last war.

'Ah there you are, Michael. Got something for you.'

He rummaged through some papers in a tray. Impatiently Mike asked, 'Is there something wrong, sir — is it my mother?'

'Good lord, no — nothing like that.'

The relief he began to feel was cut short by the adjutant's next words.

'You've been given an urgent posting — got to be on your way tonight. Got all your rail warrants here, and the transport pool have been notified to take you to the station as soon as you are ready. Ah, here we are.'

He held up a sheaf of papers.

'We shall miss you, Mike, but they're sending us a replacement, straight from Aldershot. They reckon we've got more time to absorb him than what they want you for.'

Bewildered, Mike took the papers.

'Where am I going?'

The adjutant smiled.

'Lucky you. The Isle of Wight. You are being sent to a seaborne field ambulance that is being attached to an assault brigade.'

He stood up, hand held out.

'I guess that means you are going to be in the vanguard of the invasion when it happens. Good luck, old boy.'

Mike took the proffered hand in a daze.

The realization of what it meant left him with a sick feeling in the pit of his stomach. But even worse, there was darling Lily. Would her letters ever reach him? Moving would only add complications. Miserably he went to start packing.

★   ★   ★

All the girls were in high spirits. It was the last day of the course.

Although it was the usual 0600 start, and they were outside shivering in their PT kit, the instructor for the final session was Sergeant Forster, the broad-shouldered, narrow-hipped commando dressed in his gleaming white vest and dark-blue issue shorts.

And for once, he *was* smiling.

To begin with, he clearly hadn't relished his posting to look after a lot of nurses, pretty or otherwise, when there was a war to be won.

But over the past three weeks he had relented. They had proved to be a well-co-ordinated bunch who took orders well. He didn't appreciate that after Matron, it was a piece of cake to the girls.

Suddenly he roared out and clapped his hands, making some of those in the front rank jump.

'Right, ladies, let's get on with it.'

With that he broke into an easy stride that had killed them on day one, but now they ran in little groups, the best easily keeping up with him, little realizing it was half the recommended commando speed.

As they turned out into open country, running beside the River Tweed, they could still see snow on the tops of the far-off hills.

The girl next to her shivered.

'Look at that, and it's the end of April, for God's sake.'

Soon they began to spread out, the stragglers lectured by Sergeant Forster who was running around them like a sheepdog.

For Lily, Cheltenham Ladies had been more than ample preparation, and she had been quite sporty at school. Which came in handy later when they had their final swim in the freezing outdoor pool. At least she was able to warm up, swimming back and forth. The girls who couldn't swim were blue with cold as they stood and bobbed around in the shallow end with their life jackets on.

There was one good thing they all agreed on. The food was abundant, and better than anything before. As they sat for the last lunch at the long refectory tables the girl next to her laughed.

'They're fattening us up for the slaughter.'

Lily managed to get her final letter off to Mike that day, telling him she would see him soon. As she slipped it into the postbag in the reception area she agonized for the hundredth time why she hadn't heard from him. To begin with she wondered if in the first letter she had sent, she'd forgotten to put on her address — or rather the forces post office number. Or that she'd got it wrong, she had been so tired.

But that didn't happen with all the rest — nearly two a week. It had worried her to death, so much so that she had gone to the captain, who said leave it to her, she'd try to find out if there was any reason.

Two days later she had her answer. He was still on the strength of the hospital, still working. The captain had looked at her as if to say — well, it's wartime, isn't it? He's probably dallying with another nurse now.

Lily dismissed that idea out of hand. She knew Mike — the other woman didn't.

She had complete faith in him; there must be another reason. And at least, he was all right. So she'd kept on writing, and *hoping*.

The bombshell came after lunch.

The captain walked in and called for silence.

'Ladies, you have reached the end of the course, and have been granted a night out in Edinburgh.'

There was a burst of cheering and the banging of utensils on the table.

She waited then raised a hand for silence.

'Transport will be laid on to take you to the Officers' Club there, and back, but you are free to do whatever you please. Now, tomorrow, at 1000 hours, contrary to what you might be expecting, new postings and movement orders will be issued for each of you.'

There was a stunned silence. Most thought, as did Lily, that they were going back to their own units.

The captain looked around the room from beneath her perfectly positioned peaked cap, then broke into a broad smile.

'So, enjoy yourselves while you can, but remember, girls, not all officers are gentlemen. Don't let them think you are easy.'

There was a big cheer, and some of the girls were already leaving, desperate to get to the showers first, whilst there was still hot water.

But not Lily. She was shocked by the news. Back on her bed she lay down in dejection. It was as if the gods were conspiring to keep them apart.

Lily suddenly shot up. Damn it, she would ring the hospital. She'd done it once before, but it had been a shambles and she had run out of money before she had got anywhere.

But she had to try. She scrounged and collected as many coins as she could, then raced to the wooden telephone kiosk in the old hotel lobby.

She asked the operator for the hospital number, fed in the coins and pressed button A.

After an interminable time she suddenly heard the hospital switchboard answer. The operator cut in with 'Press button B, caller'.

The line went dead as her money crashed into the box, then she asked hurriedly for 'Records Office, please.'

'Transferring you.'

Another long wait occurred. She could hear the tone ring and ring before it was picked up.

Lily knew they wouldn't give out any information willy nilly — 'Keep Mum' security and all that, but she'd thought that through.

'My name is Lieutenant de Howarth of the QAs. I need to speak to Lieutenant Gibson, a doctor on your staff, about a patient; it's very urgent. Can you give him a message to ring me back? I stress the urgency again.'

The woman hesitated, then said, 'I'm sorry, Lieutenant, he's been posted out.'

Stunned, Lily didn't answer straight away. As the beeps began again she said, 'Wait', and put in more coins. When the line came back she said, 'It's urgent, where has he gone to?'

Unseen, the woman shook her head.

'I'm afraid I couldn't give you that information, even if I knew.'

Devastated, Lily went back to her room. It was then she suddenly thought — maybe that's why he'd not written to her — he'd never received hers.

That cheered her up a bit.

The girls were all busy, hair in curlers, best underwear laid out, nails being filed; all chatty and happy.

They turned to her.

'You coming into town, Hon?'

She shook her head.

'No, I've got too much to do and letters to write.'

The girls groaned and begged. 'Oh, come on. You know it will do you good. We're all going — we should finish up celebrating together.'

'Come on. Just have a drink and a dance.'

Lily frowned. 'I don't know . . . '

There were cries from several others.

'Don't be silly. Come on, we've been cooped up here too long. A drink will do you good.'

That was the one that got her.

She really did feel the need for a drink.

Lily got her pink gin — several of them. And she did dance. A lot of the officers wore kilts, but others were in trews of the Lowland Regiments. The girls, fit as fiddles, danced non-stop, one country dance after another.

But once the band started playing smoochy numbers she went outside, onto a large terrace, lit a cigarette and leant against a stone balustrade.

It was another starry night, but no moon. She could just make out the dark shapes of the surrounding hills, and the castle towering over everything.

She remembered their walk, before they had made love.

What more could she do? Even if her letters hadn't reached him, couldn't he have found her address, if he'd *wanted* to? She felt a lump come into her throat and took a big gulp of her drink.

And now she was being sent somewhere else.

She felt tears coming into her eyes, and was glad that nobody could see her as she took out a hanky and dabbed at them.

Lily finished her cigarette, pushed the stub into a fire bucket and straightened up.

The gin had helped her, because she felt a new steely resolve.

However long it took, she would find him again.

However long it took.

10

He stood on the LCT — short for Landing Craft (Tank) — a long slab-sided steel box of a boat with a ramp designed to let down onto a beach.

The Solent was choppy, and occasionally spray came over the side but it didn't worry him any more, he'd been soaked so many times before.

He'd been on the Isle of Wight for ten days, and the tempo of their training was increasing day on day, as did the relentless build-up of the invasion force all around them.

When he'd first arrived on the final, by then, daylight leg of his journey, he'd been amazed at the number of tanks, self-propelled guns, vehicles and equipment parked in fields and woods, roads, even school playing-fields.

Now, unbelievably there were even more, blocking side streets in the towns.

Word was that two million men were involved, and it surely couldn't be long now.

He found that he was attached to a field ambulance supporting a brigade of the 3rd British Infantry Division, one of the divisions assigned for the planned attack on Hitler's Fortress Europe.

He was to form an advance dressing station link with the regimental aid posts of the assaulting battalions.

Mike realized he had been thrust into the forefront of what was going to be, one way or another, an historic battle, and was shaken by the fact, and even admitted to himself that he felt uneasy.

Would he let himself down, or the men under his command?

Another wave sprayed over the side.

He still hadn't heard from Lily. The adjutant of his old unit had promised to look into it, and if there were any letters for him, to make sure they were passed on.

Nothing.

He was brought out of his misery by the LCT starting to bump around in the shallows, lurching from side to side. Then with a roar of a diesel engine and the rattling of chains the ramp dropped onto the beach.

Immediately they swarmed out, splashing through shallow water, screamed at by their instructors to get up the beach as machine-guns firing on fixed lines sent tracer whipping over their heads.

As soon as they got to the turf beyond the pebbles they began setting up a beach dressing station, spreading out a large canvas sheet with a huge red cross on a white circle, as others put up a brown tent.

Inside, they set up drip stands, set out dressings and drugs, and used wooden packing cases as makeshift tables.

The men then practised stretcher-bearing 'casualties' from the dressing station to amphibious trucks called DUKWS which rolled up the beach, then took the 'casualties' to the large tank landing ships lying offshore where mobile theatres were set up once the tanks had gone. From there, the wounded would be taken back to England.

The exercise ended in the middle of the afternoon. They re-embarked, their LCT backing off the beach, the ramp rattling and grinding up, and then they deftly turned in a circle and headed for home.

But Mike guessed, as they all did, that it wouldn't be as easy on the day.

Whenever that would be.

That evening the camp was entertained by people from London. Jack Warner was the big name, and there were a couple of comedians and a nice line-up of girl dancers, and a singer in a glittering dress.

The men loved it, but he'd only gone because he didn't want to appear stand-offish. The men liked to see their officers in the front row, being on the end of jokes by the comedians.

Back in the mess he was nursing a whisky in both hands when he heard two colonels at the next table talking about the day's exercise.

'Needs a hell of a lot more work.'

Nodding, the other said, 'Have we got the time? With this build up it can't be far away, can it?'

Mike drained his whisky in one go and called for another one.

11

He walked into the room, across the thick carpet. She was sitting near the window, beside the grand piano. On it were dozens of silver-framed photographs, many in black and white. There was one of them on their wedding day, he still in uniform. Others, showed children, two boys and a girl, and as they grew older, in colour. There were some with them either side of mortar-boarded smiling young graduates, and then other wedding photographs, this time in colour, more babies, more children, more smiling young adults.

He reached her chair, placed his hand on her shoulder. She turned, looked up at him. It was the face he had known and loved for over fifty years.

Yet for a split second, she looked at him as if she did not know him.

Then a great big smile crossed her features and he could have cried with relief and joy.

It was short lived.

★　★　★

Lily was in Wales, outside Carmarthen, at what they had been told was a mobilization unit, to remain on standby.

There was no nursing to do. Most of the time, when they were not playing hockey, rounders and netball, they held sewing circles, sitting cross-legged outdoors, making giant red crosses to spread on the ground next to field hospitals, hopefully so enemy aircraft wouldn't bomb or strafe them.

In the evening there were lots of dances and social events at army camps and RAF airfields in the district, where the nurses were much in demand.

Lily went along, like she had in Edinburgh, but didn't protest quite so much. Being left behind in a deserted hut was a pretty miserable prospect. But guilt was there, every time a young pilot asked for a dance.

With time on their hands, they tried out the folding canvas washbowls, which proved to be very effective, both for washing and doing their laundry.

Unfortunately the folding canvas baths had a habit of collapsing with the girl in it, leaving her screaming on the grass struggling to keep her dignity as water went everywhere, much to everyone else's mirth.

But despite everything, the time dragged by. Lily felt so helpless, so miserable at the thought that it might take ages to get in touch with Mike. And if things started happening, it might be even longer.

She was sitting in the warm May sunshine when her misery came to an end.

One of the girls came past with a couple of letters in her hand.

'Oh, Hon, post is here. There's a whole pile of letters for you in the room, I saw them putting them into a packet.'

She was running before the startled girl had finished saying, 'It's early for some reason.'

Lily arrived panting at the little room that was the camp post office.

The corporal in charge looked up as she appeared, breathless, in his doorway. He knew her and said, 'Come for your mail, Ma'am?'

Eagerly Lily nodded, took the bulky service envelope and hurriedly tore it open. Her face fell with crushing disappointment as she recognized all of her old letters to Mike. It lasted until she found the note from the adjutant of his old unit, apologizing for not passing them straight onto him, but they had learnt over the years not to make assumptions, so he was returning them to her but enclosing Lieutenant Gibson's new BFPO address.

The corporal drew together the cords on the bag of mail he'd just collected.

'Excuse me, ma'am, got to get these off.'

Lily exploded into action, blocking the door, startling the man.

'Wait — oh please wait. I need to send one now.'

'I'm sorry, the driver's waiting.'

Desperately Lily looked around.

'Have you got any paper — even an envelope will do?'

Bewildered, the corporal frowned. 'Only the envelopes we use for official work.'

Lily grabbed a pencil lying on the sorting counter.

'Corporal, give me two of them. I promise you I'll only be a minute — no more — but this is desperately urgent.'

She was as good as her word. On one she wrote in a hurried scrawl her address, then:

Darling, I've found you at last. All my letters returned — will be sending them on to you so that you can see how much I love you. Darling, take care, please, please take care of yourself for me.

Postman waiting — write soon.

Your Lily. X X

Hands trembling she folded it into two, put

it into the other envelope, stuck it down and addressed it to him.

'There.'

She handed it to the now smiling corporal.

'Phew, Ma'am, he must be someone special.'

Happily she nodded. 'Yes, he is.'

Against all military codes and discipline Lily grabbed the man's cheeks in both hands and gave him a noisy kiss on the forehead.

'Thank you for waiting.'

He watched her as she almost skipped away, then franked the letter and poked it into his bag and carried it to the jeep, slinging it into the back as he swung into the passenger seat.

'OK, let's go. We'll miss the bleedin' train if we don't get a move on.'

★ ★ ★

The day had gone like any other, more of the same in the Solent, which was one massive anchorage as far as the eye could see.

On their way back in the deep water channel they ploughed their way around the big grey liberty ships and destroyers that had appeared overnight, as well as the tank landing craft moored in massed rows all across the shallower water.

There seemed to be even more activity than usual around them. He could see tanks, trucks, self-propelled guns reversing up the dropped ramps, or being swung aboard tank landing ships by derricks.

Above, silver barrage balloons wallowed in the increasing wind.

As the LCT came alongside the nearest moored LCT, he leapt across, making for the quay three ships away. When he reached it he began to pull off his lifejacket. He waved to his sergeant.

'With all this lot, Jerry must know what's up.'

The sergeant nodded.

'Doesn't know exactly where it's going though, does he, sir?'

Mike snorted. 'Neither do we.'

At the camp he checked his post. There was none. Depressed, he made his way to his room, took off his gaiters and boots and lay down on his bed, exhausted.

When he woke up, he washed, put on his shoes and wandered down to the mess to find something to eat.

He found the place humming with excitement. They had been sequestered — no movement in or out of the camp, no telephone calls, no mail, nothing. There was to be no contact with the outside world whatsoever, on the pain of court marshal.

They might as well have been on the moon.

Mike heard the term 'The balloon's gone up' more than once as he ordered a whisky. Something had tightened in the pit of his stomach.

How had he, in God's name, come to this?

It seemed like only a short while ago he'd been a student worrying about his finals. Now he was being thrust into the front line of war. No years of training for it like the rest of the army.

For a moment he felt real fear. Then he got a grip of himself, ran a hand through his hair. But what of Lily? Would he ever see her again?

He downed the last of the whisky and went out to the lobby. Little knots of officers were standing around, talking in excited tones.

He lit a cigarette, stepped out into a blustering wind. All the barrage balloons were down. It seemed unlikely weather for an invasion.

He took a drag on his cigarette. Across the bay a destroyer whooped on its siren as it prepared for sea. He thought, as he did all the time he wasn't training, about Lily. If only he had a photograph of her.

And now this.

What a rotten, sorry mess his life had

become. When he went inside a notice had been put up on the board.

He didn't have to join the throng reading it to know what it said, the word was going around. The CO was addressing them in one hour's time.

In front of the assembled field ambulance, the CO announced that D-Day had been set for the 5 June.

Tomorrow, the 4 June, they would be embarking at 1600 hours.

They were to be issued with 48-hour ration packs, including fifty cigarettes and some chocolate, and an amount of British Liberation Army money, to be spent in France. Its value was backed by the Allies, as it was likely that the currency of the German occupation could well collapse.

The men could only take their pay book, part one, and the Holy Bible with them.

Everything else had to be put in the large envelopes provided, to be sent back home, but that wouldn't happen for at least a week. Any other material had to be burnt. Large fires were being lit for this purpose. On a more sinister note, the CO reminded them they should all make their wills, the men using form B2089, officers' copies were available from the adjutant's office.

He finished by announcing that in the two

Nissen huts by the mess hall there were now large maps and photographs of the exact part of the Normandy coast where they would be going in at H-hour + 1. Normandy — so that was their destination.

There were details of the landing beach, and assembly points if they were split up.

'Memorize them, gentlemen, it could make the difference to what happens to you.'

'Happens to you' seemed to hang in the air.

He spent some time looking at the maps of the beach, and the assembly points, making notes. Afterwards, he went for an early supper, suddenly finding himself ravenous.

He smiled, nature kicking in. After the fear, the survival instinct.

Mike picked up a will form, and left the £94 he had managed to save, to his mother.

He also wrote a letter to her, trying to reassure her by saying that he would probably be seeing her in the not too distant future. He sealed both into the envelope as directed.

With that done his thoughts returned once more to Lily.

Mike had no address for her, but if anything happened to him, he wanted there to be some record of his last words to her. He sat for some time, eyes closed, remembering the short time they had had together, especially the one night they had been all alone in the world.

He began to write.

Darling Lily

Whatever happens in the next few days I just want you to know that you brought untold happiness into my life, in fact, it was only with you that I really became a man — in the best sense of the word.

Nothing that happened before I met you now seems to matter.

I love you so deeply that, frankly, the pain of not being with you, not knowing where you are, never leaves me.

My fervent prayer is that we will be reunited once again in this lifetime. If that is not to be, please remember that you have been loved with all my heart, but you must move on, life is too precious to be wasted. Find a man who will love you and take care of you as I would have, and give you the children you should have — and the career you so desire.

I take with me the most wonderful memories, and if anything happens, please know you made me the happiest man in the world.

With all my love
Mike

He sat for a long time staring at it, then suddenly folded the sheet, placed it in the envelope and put her name on it: Lieutenant Lily de Howarth. Queen Alexandra Imperial Military Nursing Service.

And in the top corner, in bold capitals — URGENT. TO BE FORWARDED — ADDRESS UNKNOWN.

12

'Hello, Darling.'

He leant down to kiss her. It happened so quickly, he could never get used to it.

The smiling blue eyes suddenly blazed with hostility and fear, and her arm came up protectively, knocking his aside.

'How dare you? What do you think you are doing?' She started shouting. 'Help. Help. I don't know you, I don't know you.'

He tried to calm her down.

'Ssh, sssh, darling, it's me, Mike.'

'I don't know anybody called Mike. I don't, I don't.'

She started to cry.

Slowly, fearful that she would become violent again, he put out his arms, and gradually brought her to him. He felt the bones of her body, as he soothed her.

'There there, darling.'

She didn't feel the tears dropping gently onto her hair.

★ ★ ★

Lily had still heard nothing from him.

Her initial euphoria had slowly dissipated. Now, she was if anything, more desperate than ever.

He *must* have got her letter, so why hadn't he replied?

It was beginning to eat away at her and, to cap it all, that morning her period had started.

Depressed, she joined her friends for breakfast, setting down her tray with its mug of tea and a plate with a greasy-looking omelette made of powdered egg onto the table.

They all exchanged greetings, but nobody was in good form. Time was beginning to drag heavily. Nothing was happening; the war seemed to be on hold. They knew that it wouldn't always be so, but morale was beginning to slip.

They'd finished eating and were passing cigarettes around when one of them said, 'Is it me, but where are all the doctors?'

One of the girls waved out of the window.

'Well, there's two. What do you mean?'

The girl shrugged.

'They just seem to be short on the ground this morning. I wondered if there was an exercise on or something.'

Somebody said, 'I've not heard of anything.'

Lily, too, had noticed there had been very few doctors when she had been on her morning run, but had thought nothing of it.

Slowly she stood up.

'You're right. I wonder what's going on?'

Rumours began to circulate. Had the invasion started?

It was noticed not a single nurse was missing, only RAMC officers.

By lunchtime the excitement was rife. People gathered round the wireless for the news — but it was not what they were expecting. Nevertheless, there was excitement — Rome had fallen to the Allies.

The only person who seemed unmoved was Matron, who remained as stony-faced as ever.

The day passed and ended in disappointment. And by then the rain was lashing down on the window as Lily lay on her bed, cigarette in hand. She watched the smoke drift lazily upwards as the drops trickled down the window pane.

Was he in danger?

She couldn't even worry properly: she just had no idea what was happening, or where he was.

Lily had never felt so helpless before. And for the first time ever, she stubbed out the cigarette, turned on her side, and cried gently

118

into her pillow. Sleep only came in the early hours.

A troubled sleep.

She dreamed of Mike. He was standing on a beach, with his back to her, but she knew it was him.

She shouted, screamed, pleaded, but he would not turn around, would not come to her.

★　★　★

With beer mugs in their hands a crowd had formed around the piano in the mess. As Mike walked in they were roaring out *Run, rabbit, run, rabbit, run, run, run.* He stayed for a while, but after a rendering of *We'll Meet Again* he drifted away. They were obviously getting sentimental, and he didn't think he could stand that in the circumstances. He played cards for a while, and then in a largely deserted mess, listened to one of the chaps playing Chopin's Nocturne in E flat.

It sent him to bed feeling sad, thinking of all those young men in the war-to-end-all-wars who had listened to it in the parlours of Edwardian homes, with the soft gaslight picking out the aspidistra, and a young girl at the piano. Then they had marched off to war and had never heard it again.

He was awakened to the usual bustle of men getting ready for the day — a rather special day he remembered with a jolt, shaving, showering, pulling on battledress trousers and buttoning up battledress blouses.

At breakfast, a special church service was announced. Mike wasn't particularly religious, having attended Sunday school and church rather irregularly, but in the circumstances . . .

When he turned up, the attendance was more than anything he'd seen before.

The padre made it simple, and fast.

He knew his audience, foxhole religion it was called, and he had a tight schedule to keep with all the other units he was visiting. After it was over the CO came forward and held up a hand to stop them dispersing.

'Stay where you are. We have a surprise for you. One I think you are going to enjoy.'

Mike heard one of the men mutter, 'Oh, yeah, well, I've had enough of bloody surprises, thank you very much.'

But stay he did.

It was a whirlwind visit, lasting no more than twenty minutes. Like the padre he had a lot to do that day.

And it was informal.

He moved amongst them, sitting on the back of an open car as they gathered around, cheering. He waved, raised his Homburg hat, and took the cigar from his mouth as he gave his famous 'V' for Victory sign.

'Who's the bloke with Winnie?' somebody asked.

They didn't know, so Mike turned and said, 'That's Jan Smuts, the South African general.'

Churchill wished them God speed, and a safe return, then his little convoy moved off. The last hot meal was served to the troops before embarkation began. Queues of other ranks formed as the catering corps handed out mugs of steaming tea and doled out hot stew into the held mess tins. Mike, as orderly officer moved among them.

Just hearing their cheerful banter and fatalistic humour helped to release the tension.

'If it's got your name on it, Spud, can I have your ukulele?'

'Smoking will stop your growth, boyo, you'd better give me your ration.'

'Die in battle, die of boredom — what's the difference?'

But there was no denying the undercurrent of fear of the unknown.

When it was his turn to eat, Mike found his

stomach didn't feel good, but he forced himself. It was going to be some time before they would get a proper hot meal again.

After that there was a final check of their equipment — syringes, suture packets, surgical kits, tourniquets, transfusion kits, swabs, antiseptic bottles, dressing packs, serum and saline bottles. As he went through it his sergeant ticked them off a list, and they were repacked by the rest of the team in their carrying cases.

Just as they finished, some of the units started passing by towards the docks. There were waves and handshakes and calls of 'Well, this is it. See you on the other side.'

Mike shook several hands, exchanged 'Good lucks'. While they waited there were frequent trips to the lavatories.

The time finally came for them to board. The marshalling officer and his sergeant came along with his clipboard.

'Right. You're next. Start moving.'

★   ★   ★

They had been on board for hours, listening to the whoops of the destroyers as they put to sea. It was dark before they began to move, backing out into a choppy sea, joining others moving slowly down the Solent. As they moved out from the shelter of the coast, the waves grew bigger.

But it was when they passed the Needles that conditions grew markedly worse, and there was a real fear among the soldiers that the box-like LCT, loaded with three tanks and other vehicles, was wallowing and taking water in an alarming manner.

Many of his men were too ill to care, the bilges running with vomit.

Not long afterwards the ship changed direction, and the word soon spread that they had been recalled. How they could have attempted a landing in these conditions he did not know.

It was eventually confirmed: D-Day had been postponed. Hours later they made it back to their berth.

But further agony was to come. They were not going to be disembarked, but had to stay on board for a further twenty-four hours. Groaning, they tried to get some sleep. Those who felt like it were told they could eat their ration packs — others would be provided.

A dreadful anticlimax pervaded the entire ship. All morning the wind blew and rain came in squalls, but by four o'clock the gale began to ease slightly, and the rain stopped.

In the early evening the signal came through. It was for a 'go' for the 6th. The risk had been assessed and the standing down of nearly two million troops for another month, and the need to keep security, had been balanced against a relative calm period forecast to be coming in from the Atlantic. They knew nothing of the agonizing decision the supreme commander had had to take. All they knew was that it was still bloody rough.

This time there was no great feeling of excitement as the engines rumbled into action once more, and they began to move off their mooring.

The sea was still running, and they all dreaded the misery that the next hours would bring.

As if to add insult to injury, over the tannoy, playing music to try and cheer them up came 'Someone's rocking my Dreamboat'.

There was booing and jeering. Despite the Hyoscine tablets they had been given to try and suppress the sickness, the further out into the Channel they went the more the LCT began rolling like a barrel. This time Mike joined everybody else being ill. The craft was awash with vomit.

Hours later and the tannoy announced they were closing with the French coast. The sea was becoming less and less rough, but his nausea continued, the stress of what was to come gaining with every lumbering wallow they took nearer the enemy shore.

The sky began to lighten in the east, and with it came the first sight of the massive armada all around them.

Mike was taken aback by the black shapes of hundreds and hundreds of ships of all sizes, from battleships and cruisers, to the smallest assault craft, stretching in every direction to the horizon.

Barrage balloons filled the sky, tethered to ships, and above them he could see and hear scores of aircraft, all heading for France. The sight of the invasion force made him feel better. It looked invincible.

Suddenly the dawn was stabbed by hundreds of flashes, followed in seconds by the most tremendous thunder of guns that made the ship shudder with the shock waves of the detonations.

'Jesus.' His sergeant thrust his hands over his ears as the awesome noise continued. The huge sixteen-inch naval guns of the battle-ships and monitors sent shells that roared like express trains overhead, while rocket ships fired salvo after salvo of fiery projectiles into the dawn sky.

The noise was physically overpowering. How could anything live on the receiving end of such a storm?

Flames and dust rose in the air where the

coastline of Normandy lay, still several miles away.

They all began to feel better.

In the steadily increasing light they could see men of the assault waves climbing down the scrambling nets on the sides of the bigger troopships, getting into the infantry landing craft, which then began circling until the formation was ready.

Still under the enormous non-stop thunder of the naval bombardment, the assault boats went line abreast and headed for the shore, close enough now for the outlines of houses and churches and pill boxes to be seen.

More boats followed the first wave as their own engines settled back and their headway decreased.

Mike could see their wavy navy petty officer on the bridge situated towards the stern, looking through binoculars.

It took twenty minutes for the first assault craft to hit the beach, and then, just as their own barrage began to lift, muzzle flashes rippled all along the shore as the enemy guns opened up on the first wave of troops wading through the sea around the mined obstacles sticking out of the sand. Soon a yellowish fog swathed the scene, and nothing could be seen except the continuing muzzle flashes and tracer as the battle raged.

Mike looked from it back to his men. Their faces looked white, tense, frightened. He knew his must be the same.

Their boat seemed to be almost at a standstill, wallowing in the waves that hissed by heading for the beach.

No information was relayed to them, but he could see the mounting congestion of the ships and boats all around, and guessed it must be due to that.

From a battleship far behind them another salvo screamed overhead, as a destroyer edged its way nearer to the shore, its guns firing almost horizontally, blasting the enemy beach defences. More infantry assault boats began heading into the inferno, and then their own engines roared into life, and once more they were moving steadily forward, other LCTs on either side forming another wave about to beach on the shore of Hitler's Fortress Europe.

Geysers of water began to spout up and fall back in the sea all around them.

Mike looked at them almost disinterestedly, until all of a sudden he had to duck as, with a whistle, a shell landed alongside, the explosion blowing a gale of water over the side drenching them all. Others followed as they crouched down, pressed hard against the steel side plates.

Up in the exposed high bridge of the LCT he could see the skipper and the wavy navy sub-lieutenant who was navigating them to their designated landing point, together with the coxswain at the wheel, carrying on unperturbed.

Suddenly sailors were shouting and pointing over the side. There were men struggling in the water. The skipper used a megaphone to address the agitated men.

'Our orders of the day are to make for the beach, not to stop, not to pick up survivors. We have to get to the beach.'

In horror they watched the struggling men go past, ending up bobbing in their wake.

His sergeant breathed out, 'God help them.'

They started to go through wreaths of black smoke. The rattle of machine gun fire became almost non-stop. The boat seemed to be going faster, and he realized they were in shallow water, running in on the incoming tide. A mass of dead bodies, lifeless arms and legs rising and falling with the waves, swirled about in the hissing water.

Now he could see, close up, the metal and wood beach obstacles and the attached mines.

Strange swishing and pinging noises began. One of his men spun around, screaming as blood spurted from his shoulder. Only then did he realize they were under sniper fire.

With a juddery clunk they hit an obstacle, the mine exploding blowing a hole in the landing ramp. Seawater surged in and their forward motion ground to a halt. Instantly the two sailors manning the winch motor on the port side started to let down the ramp. A shell struck the water beside them. When the blast had cleared, shrapnel had taken away half the head of one of them who lay twisted up on the deck. It was awash with blood.

Unscathed the other stayed at his post. The ramp splashed down, but the beach was still some way off.

The LCTs 30mm Oerlikon gun kept up a thunderous fire as the first Sherman tank, pouring clouds of blue diesel smoke lumbered down into the sea, which surged over it, before it reared up again, water streaming off the casing. A second was following when a shell struck the wheelhouse, and ricocheted around the interior before exploding.

The skipper was blown out onto the deck, the wavy navy lieutenant lay screaming on the wheelhouse floor, both legs gone above the knee, white bone sticking out of the brilliant red of pumping arterial blood. The coxswain's lifeless body lay over the remains of the wheel. Two of his men rushed to help the sub-lieutenant, and were still working on him when it was the turn of the medics to disembark.

Shouted and screamed at, they were urged out into the open, away from the shelter of the steel hull. Mike started yelling, he didn't know why. He jumped off the end of the ramp — and went over his head into ice-cold water.

Beside him, his sergeant and a corporal, moving a Miller James stretcher on wheels, floundered. The carrier overturned, and the equipment cases on it fell off and floated away. They all struggled to retrieve them, aware of the full horror unfolding around them.

Sappers, pouring out of the LCT alongside theirs were flung about as machine-gun fire swept through them. Jolting like rag dolls they clutched at their bodies, then sank out of sight beneath the waves.

It was carnage. Clusters of bodies bobbed around the mined obstacles that stood out like ragged teeth in the sea.

A beach-master was screaming at them to 'Keep moving, keep moving!'

A sudden flurry of mortar shells began bursting around them, one showering him with mud and water. As they got further into the shallows they came under intense sniper fire.

Bullets whined around their heads like angry bees, thumping into the sands.

Wrecked infantry landing craft lay at the water's edge, some still with troops aboard — dead or dying. Beyond, on the beach, more were strewn around screaming and begging for 'stretcher bearers'.

As they crouched down to deal with the injured, two beach commandos appeared, hauling at their arms, getting them onto their feet again.

'Don't stop. Get up the beach, get up the beach. Follow the tanks. Keep moving.'

Nearby an LCT coming in hit a mine. It blew the ramp off, slewing the vessel to one side, but the Sherman inside ground over the twisted metal and lumbered through the shallows to roar past them, almost disappearing into the smoke.

'Come on — get behind.'

He led the way, crouching in the shelter afforded by the steel hulk, which was already firing at the German 88mm guns, its own mounted machine-guns raking the unseen dunes and pill boxes. They moved further forward, passing a tank on fire, one of several causing the billowing smoke that was still making them choke and their eyes burn. But

Mike realized that it was making it difficult for the snipers and machine-gunners to see them clearly.

It seemed a huge, never-ending beach, but suddenly they came out of the smoke to find themselves near the pebble line, and the seafront houses.

As their tank, its machine-guns still blazing, slewed away to the left, they ran for the low sea wall. No enemy fire came their way. The first line of the German defence had been broken, they could see their tanks moving inland further along the shore.

They stayed where they were, getting their breath back, coughing and spluttering, as they watched the senior beach-master, a navy lieutenant commander and his staff trying to make order out of the chaos as more vehicles, tanks, half-trucks, and jeeps poured into the beach-head. Eventually they looked at each other.

Not a word was spoken. They didn't have to. Mike knew what they were thinking. He was too.

How bloody wonderful it was to be alive.

13

It was 9.30 a.m. Lily was with the others, finishing a late breakfast, the wireless playing dance music over the speakers set on the walls.

They were all moaning about their continued inactivity, and still wondering about the missing RAMC doctors.

Some girls, just back from leave in London had reported that the Allied servicemen who normally thronged the streets of the West End, especially around Piccadilly had disappeared overnight.

Another girl, who had gone home to the East End, said that the lower Thames, previously crowded with landing craft, was now empty.

They carried on talking, because there was nothing for them to do. It was beginning to really get to them, some even talking about trying to get a transfer. Suddenly the music ceased, halfway through the melody, the silence broken only by a crackling hiss.

They all stopped talking, instinctively looking up at the twin brown speakers placed near the ceiling, expecting an announcement from the CO.

A voice broke the silence.

'*This is the BBC Home Service broadcast.*'

There was a pause and then: '*Early this morning the Allies began the assault on the north western face of Hitler's Fortress Europe, and here is a special bulletin read by John Snagg —* '

When it finished the girls stood up as one, cheering and hugging each other.

Lily, eventually, slowly, sat back down again.

Mike? Was he involved? Was he in danger?

She'd have given the whole world to know what he was doing right then.

★   ★   ★

They'd eventually joined the columns of marching infantry and armoured vehicles heading inland. Past a row of shattered and burning seaside villas they turned off into an orchard, their assembly point before being called forward to set up the advance dressing station.

Mike slumped down with the rest of them, pulling off his steel helmet and running a hand through his sweat-soaked hair.

He looked at his hand. It had a tremor. In the flap pocket of his battledress trousers he found a bag of boiled sweets, took them out and shared them around. The lemon taste cut into his painfully cracked, dry mouth.

With a whoosh a shell exploded nearby. They flung themselves flat on the ground as an infantry major bellowed, 'You, medics — dig in, you bloody fools!'

They needed no second encouragement. In no time they had scraped out several shallow trenches.

Word had got around that they were a medical unit. Casualties began arriving, some on stretchers, others supported by comrades.

His sergeant started to turn them away.

'We're not set up — waiting for orders.'

Another shell whistled down, even closer. Mike jumped into one of the trenches as the rest rolled into the others.

The ground leapt upwards, jarring into his face, followed by a hail of sand and stones on his back. Somewhere close by someone was screaming, 'Help me, help me!'

Haunted by the casualties they had had to leave behind on the beach, Mike stood up, brushing the sand from his uniform, and wiping a sleeve across his face to clear his eyes, and made a quick decision.

'Right, get out the red cross. We'll start our war here — where we're needed.'

★ ★ ★

135

Whilst the rest carried on celebrating, Lily went outside, stood in the sunshine, but it was still breezy.

She lit a cigarette, having to cup her hands to stop the flame of the lighter blowing out. The cool taste of the smoke steadied her nerves.

It was then she remembered her letter. She prayed that he had received it. If anything happened to him —

The breeze lifted her hair wildly around her face and into her eyes.

That was why they were wet, she told a friend who'd come outside and found her, the strong forceful Hon who cared for nothing, feared nobody — well, Matron excepted — dabbing at her eyes with her handkerchief.

The girl wasn't fooled. She had been crying. It must be that young lieutenant she was so nonchalant about. People had teased her after seeing her with him.

Lily had a restless night, but next morning nobody had time to mope or think of themselves. It had happened.

The news went around the camp like wildfire: orders had been posted. At last they were on the move. Even Lily felt a sense of relief. The awful boredom was over.

They drove to the station in a convoy of three-tonners, passing villagers who waved and cheered them on.

At the station, as they were forming up on the forecourt, three Spitfires from the RAF station where they had enjoyed many a social occasion, flew low overhead, wagging their wings in a farewell salute.

Much to the Matron's horror many of the girls cheered and waved, some more emotional than others.

The train got underway, but would take all of that day and half the next, as goods train after goods train full of armaments and vehicles took priority over them, forcing them to wait, sometimes even shunted into sidings for hours on end.

The weather was rough again as they eventually reached their destination, a grand eighteenth-century house close to Portsmouth which, they were told, would be their embarkation port as soon as conditions over in France were right.

Exhausted, they were not allowed to rest. The field hospital equipment had to be rechecked and then loaded onto the trucks that would eventually cross the channel with them, before they were released. Dog-tired, Lily reached her room in the old servant's quarters of the house at six o'clock in the evening. By then, the news bulletins were reporting heavy fighting in France, but the

Allies had achieved a bridgehead several miles deep. She slept, thoughts about Mike mixed with the excitement at what was awaiting them on the other side of the channel.

★　★　★

Blue sky, wonderful, peaceful, wide, blue sky. He lay on his back, arms behind his head, revelling in the rare inactivity, and the quietness after the non-stop thunder of the guns.

The previous weeks had seen intense fighting as the British thrust for Caen had become bogged down.

The Germans were resisting with the same ferocity and fighting spirit they had shown at Monte Cassino. It could only be admired, if cursed.

He reflected on his work. Already he was something of a veteran battlefield MO. As the Guards Armoured Division had tried to press forward, the casualty clearing station had been inundated with wounded.

There had been horrible burns and blast injuries, the like he had never seen in civilian life. The first was a sergeant who had been brought in with a face that was a bloody mess, half of it hanging down onto his neck, his eye fallen onto where his cheek should have been.

He'd given the moaning, frothing patient morphine then rolled up some lint into a wedge and put it onto the mouth cavity and pulled the face back into place, securing it with five safety pins. Over that he'd wound more bandages and used plasters to hold everything in place. With a shot of the new drug, penicillin, he'd send him back to the beach, where the amphibious DUKWs were ferrying the injured out to the Landing Ships Tanks lying off the beaches, that were taking them back to Blighty.

There followed a never-ending stream of horrendous injuries, and he was lost in the routine of stemming blood flow, treating shock, administering morphine, setting up drips and transfusions, replacing field dressings, giving sulphonamides and the new penicillin.

Then had come a momentous change, for him.

The regimental MO of one of the Guards battalions had reached some woods with his team, only to find it was still occupied by the enemy. He was taken prisoner, and Mike had been ordered forward with several men of his section to replace them.

On their way they had passed through a

bombed, still burning village, giving a cheery wave to the few French people they passed. For the most part they were ignored. One spat in their direction, but this was made up for by an elderly man who insisted on sharing his bottle of very rough Calvados with them.

Now, as he lay there, the war had mysteriously, wonderfully, gone away. The guns had fallen strangely silent, and the constant stream of wounded had miraculously dried to a trickle of minor injuries that his sergeant was treating.

In fact, it was the men who had told him to go and have a rest.

He lay down between an apple tree and a hawthorn hedge, beside some wild flowers. Bees droned past his head, and he could hear grasshoppers chirping in the long grass. Otherwise, the land was silent. There was no bird song, no rabbits scampering about. Only the insects held sway.

The stench emanating from the hundreds of dead cows, bellies hugely swollen and distorted with gas, lay heavy in the air. Every now and then one of the animals exploded, followed by a hissing sound as the gas and entrails slid out.

In the beginning, the troops had used them for target practice, but the smell as the bullets burst the distended abdomens had put paid to that.

Another bee droned by.

He wondered why there was such a lull. Perhaps that happened in war; he had no experience — thank God.

It couldn't last.

And it didn't.

That evening, as they were eating their rations and brewing tea, a steady roaring sound began to build. To begin with they assumed a column of tanks was coming up the lane to reinforce them.

Then the first Lancaster came flying over them, followed by wave after wave after wave of the giant four-engined aircraft.

Seconds later, the bombs began to fall on Caen.

The earth shook, the can over their fire fell over, the flames hissing in the water. The air seemed to be sucked out of their lungs. Then their tent collapsed, leaves, branches, apples rained down on them as they reeled around, stumbling into each other.

Mike slumped to the damp earth and put both arms around a tree trunk and held on grimly as the ground spasmed with the non-stop detonations.

Above the tree-line, the whole sky was ablaze with yellow and white light, reflecting on the vast clouds of smoke and dust rising into the clear sky above the city.

The day after, the resistance at Caen ceased.

★   ★   ★

Lily had just tramped in her army boots down the grand staircase of the house and was on her way to get her breakfast in the ballroom, when she came upon the crowd milling about before the noticeboard in the hall.

Coming away, one of the girls was walking past her. Lily grabbed her arm.

'What is it?'

The girl's eyes were shining.

'We're moving tomorrow — to the docks.'

Lily suddenly found it difficult to breathe. At last it had finally come. They were going to war.

Throughout the day the excited girls packed their personal belongings and the boxes and placed them in the hall.

Men of the RASC collected them and loaded them into the trucks that were taking all the equipment for the field hospital on ahead.

'It's France, of course, couldn't be much doubt about that, could there?' said Matron, as she addressed them in the ballroom. 'You will be issued with twenty-four hours of emergency rations. This will include solid cubes of tea, milk and sugar combined.'

Somebody said 'ugh' and there was laughter, quickly silenced by Matron's look.

The list continued. There were flapjacks, hard chocolate, a Billycan, and four cigarettes — which could be swapped if they wished.

Matron looked around severely, determined to nip any hilarity in the bud before it began as she said, 'Four pieces of lavatory paper are included as you will be operating in the field.'

At that the girls couldn't contain themselves. Impatiently, Matron waited before going on, 'You will also be entitled to government issue sanitary towels.'

The girl next to Lily whispered, 'I'm not taking any chances on that, I've got my own packets — lots of them.'

They were also entitled to take a comb, lipstick and some hankies in the same packs.

In the evening, in full battle gear of steel helmets, gaiters and webbing they climbed aboard the convoy of trucks that had come for them.

Their journey took them through a countryside still packed with an invading army's needs: tanks, trucks, ordnance. Seeing them the girls' mood became quieter.

Eventually they reached where they were staying for the night, another hutted camp where they were given hot stew, which they took outside and sat in the open to eat.

Afterwards someone played a mouth organ, and coins were tossed into an upturned tin hat, which were used to buy some drinks.

Nobody slept much for the few hours before dawn and then they were on their way again. By eight o'clock the field hospital had embarked on a troopship, the girls waving to the amazed dockers who stopped to watch all these women going off to war.

Once they were underway they assumed they would be in France within hours, but they lay off the coast of England all day. It was nightfall before they began their journey across the Channel.

Lying on their uncomfortable bunks they were under strict orders not to undress, and to keep their lifejackets at hand all the time. They took it in turns to go up on deck and get some fresh air.

Lily was on her bunk when the sound of the ship's siren, the clomping of feet on the deck above her cabin and the realization that the sound of the engines had decreased alerted her to the fact that they had arrived in France.

The sight that confronted her as she emerged on deck was of the floating harbour they had all heard and read about in the newspapers called Mulberry.

They were at Arromanches.

All around were hundreds of ships bringing over a never-ending supply of matériel.

Lily felt great pride that the Allies could bring such might to bear.

They disembarked down the gangplanks, weighed down with their tin hats on their heads, gas masks around their necks, kitbags over their shoulders.

As they reached the floating pontoons with loose planks of wood on top, men shouted at them to watch their footing.

There was no sound of war, but the air still stank of cordite and burning, and the occasional bloated body swirled around in the water as boats manoeuvred to unload.

Some of the girls looked green at the sight and it brought home to Lily the awful danger Mike might be in — if he was over here, but she still had no idea where he was.

When they got to the line of waiting trucks, their transport to the site of the hospital, a great cheer went up.

Men shouted to others.

'Girls, we've got girls coming over.'

'Hey sweethearts. How are things in England?'

'Has anybody got a newspaper?'

'Wouldn't have any white bread, would you?'

The girls laughed. Commissioned or not, it was a welcome relief to be among the ordinary Tommies again.

The convoy wound its way out of the beach area, through ruined buildings and burnt-out tanks strewn everywhere — signs of the intense battles that had taken place.

On the way to Bayeux they passed a field full of broken gliders, which had brought over the airborne troops. The town itself was almost all rubble.

As they got nearer to the site, they heard for the first time, far off, the dull rumble of guns, which sent a shiver down many a back. Their tents and the big red crosses were already up as they turned in down the muddy track.

The guns were soon forgotten as, for the first time in days, they were able to undress properly, including the bliss of getting their socks off, and having a good wash.

On that first night in France, Lily lay on her cot and wondered if Mike was near. Maybe he was only a few miles away.

As she turned over, her cot creaking, she made her mind up. Even if it was daft she would start asking everybody who she came into contact with, if they knew him or had heard about him.

They had been warned they would be busy. For the first time in forty-eight hours she slept deeply, not even disturbed by the guns which became louder, more persistent.

They would, indeed, be busy in the morning.

14

He hugged her for some time, until her bony, emaciated body stopped trembling. He stroked her hair, whispered gently until she was calm, and then he eased her slowly away from him.

Hope sprang eternal that she would somehow, miraculously, be better, that there would be true recognition in those, now not so blue, eyes.

But it was not to be.

She smiled at him vacantly, didn't even react when he started to sob.

He was angry for her.

He was angry for himself.

He was crying for them both.

★ ★ ★

When they eventually drove through the ruins of Caen, Mike couldn't see a single building standing or untouched. How could anybody have survived? But survive they had.

A few older men and women, dressed in black, were sifting through the wreckage looking for anything of value.

Down the road, they had already passed a couple of women with hammers and chisels and a bucket, knocking the gold teeth out of the German dead.

Columns of black smoke rose in the air from burning buildings and several blackened carcasses of German tiger tanks, still with flames licking from under the engine bays, were half buried in fallen bricks. By a shattered church they came across rows and rows of French civilian dead. The price of freedom. As was the sight of several terrified women, heads shaved, with placards around them reading *Collaboratrice* being goaded and pushed along by a jeering crowd.

Out on the other side of the town, the retreating Germans were being encircled at a place called Falaise.

They were driving along a road in that direction, behind a column of tanks of the Irish Guards, when out of the sky several white trails dropped swiftly around them. The explosions were enormous, blowing the jeep over onto two wheels. As it bounced back, the driver got it under control and pulled into the verge.

Sounds like banshees came again as they threw themselves into a deep ditch. The mortar trails ended in more explosions in the field beside them.

'Bloody Moaning Minnies,' came from somewhere deep in the ditch.

Mike had heard the expression and knew it was the squaddies' nickname for the feared multiple mortars the Germans called *Nebel-werfers*. He had never been on the receiving end before and, as another salvo came over, he put both hands on top of his steel helmet, held it hard down, and buried his face in the wet ground. The earth shuddered, and bits of rock and mud rained down on his back.

'Christ.'

Shortly afterwards they heard aircraft engines, high in the sky at first, then getting louder and rising into a scream as they dived on their target.

Two tremendous *crumps* shook the ground.

They waited. No more Moaning Minnies came over.

Slowly they climbed out of the ditch. Further down the road a house was burning.

'The bastards.'

Startled, Mike turned to find his driver looking at their sleeping tent rolled into its bag on the jeep.

It was in shreds.

A week later and Mike came face to face with his first German casualties as the destruction of the enemy forces in the Falaise pocket, as it was now called, gathered pace.

The first was a major, who asked in excellent English for a cigarette as they tried to staunch the flow of blood from a gaping wound in his thigh.

Mike gave him one of his and lit it for him.

The German nodded his thanks and inhaled deeply. When he blew out the smoke he looked at the glowing tip and sighed.

'I haven't tasted good Virginia tobacco for years.'

With a pressure pack on they sent him back down the line. Mike pondered, there were decent Germans after all.

But not long after that they were treating a young trooper of the 2nd SS Division, setting up a blood transfusion, when the young blond shot out a hand, grabbed his arm, and said, '*Nein.*'

Puzzled, through an interpreter they explained he could well die if he didn't let them do it.

The reply was unbelievable.

'It may be Jewish blood.'

The orderly, who drove him back to the clearing station on a jeep stretcher-carrier, reported that he had died on the way.

Mike shook his head in despair at the fanatical nature at the heart of the enemy resistance.

It didn't bode well for those who said it

would all be over by Christmas.

After one particularly heavy intake of casualties, he took time out, found a fence, slumped down against a post, and took out his cigarettes.

Behind him was the ripening corn in the late August sunshine. He slapped his arm as one of the myriad of mosquitoes landed on his skin.

He lit up, breathed in the first lungful of smoke, then eased it slowly out through his nostrils. In the past three months he had changed, all of them had changed. Since they had waded ashore they had seen too much, heard too much, smelt too much to be the same people.

It was a loss of innocence. Innocence? He thought of that night he and Lily had shared — remembered her touch, her taste, her soft whispers of delight.

It seemed so long ago — another lifetime almost, so much had changed since then. He knew he had aged, in a way that war ages young men. Would Lily still love him?

Had she ever loved him? Why had he not heard from her by now? Then he dismissed that, angry with himself for ever doubting her.

He *knew* what they had both felt: knew that she loved him.

He suddenly gave out a big sob.

It took him completely by surprise. Embarrassed he looked around, frightened that they would think he was breaking up, but everybody was going about their business — lathering and shaving, braces around their waists, others brewing tea, cleaning instruments, restocking the packs.

Relieved, he pulled on his cigarette.

Lily, Lily, what had happened to her?

Would they ever meet again in this lifetime?

★ ★ ★

The object of his anguish was only several kilometres away. Her field hospital was set, like so many, among the apple orchards of Normandy, on the road between Bayeux and Caen. The forty large olive-green tents had big white circles on the roofs inset with large red crosses. So many hospitals were now in place on both sides of the road, that the area had become known as Harley Street.

Soon after they had arrived, torrential rain had begun, turning all the tracks into deep mud, which even flowed over the tarpaulin floors of the wards.

Now, the blazing August sun had baked everything brick hard, and flies and mosquitoes were a constant menace.

153

The Pioneer Corps had set up the operating tables on concrete floats in the middle of the theatre tents, two to each one, so the surgeons worked back to back. Generators gave light to the theatres and main areas — but wards and living quarters had hurricane lamps.

Lily, too, had changed.

After all the months of inactivity they had been almost overwhelmed with work. Instead of being the large base hospital that had been intended, because of the fierce German resistance at Caen and now Falaise, the planned advance had stalled, and they had ended up operating to the limit of their resources as a 600-bed casualty station — taking wounded straight from the front.

The thunder of the guns was an almost continuous background, and when anti-aircraft guns arrived and were positioned in the next field, the noise was appalling — they had to shout at each other even as the surgeons were operating.

Although they had other duties, handed out daily by Matron, Lily was usually in charge of one of the pre-op tents, including resuscitation and the stocks of blood and saline.

The first time she started work — their first intake of wounded — had been dramatic and shocking, a brutal introduction to the surgery of war. The ambulances had come bumping and grinding across the tracks, and begun to unload their bloody contents.

Lily, bursting forward to help was startled to find the men still clinging to their rifles — and grenades.

That first wave had almost overwhelmed them. There were always men on stretchers waiting in her tent to be next on the table. Exhausted, the surgeons were only just able to cope.

It was here that the young Lily had also been changed forever.

The men — boys, really, as some were only eighteen or nineteen — had had dreadful injuries: chests split wide open, with ribs sticking up like a wrecked boat, entrails spilling or blown clean away, limbs torn off, genitals missing. Land mines and shrapnel accounted for most of the horrendous wounds.

The carnage of war.

Covered in mud and oil and living in foxholes with no toilet paper they had to be cleaned before surgery, but to keep them warm because of shock, they only cut away the part of their uniform where the wound was located. Lily had found that things happened differently in a field hospital. The surgeons left wounds open, and amputation stumps were not covered with a flap of skin because of the risk of gangrene from the infection carried into the body.

There were no sheets on the beds, just army blankets. The sheets were reserved for the theatres. Bottles for transfusions they tied to guy ropes or anywhere else handy.

She had just finished a cup of tea when the bugle that always heralded the arrival of the injured blew a long note of warning.

She ran, with all the other nurses on duty, to meet the long line of ambulances. The doors opened and the orderlies began unloading the stretchers.

Lily started checking the labels tied to a button hole on their battledress blouses, detailing the treatment that had already been given and when.

Yellow labels showed that they had had the new wonder drug penicillin, red ones, the standard sulphonamide to fight infection. On their foreheads in indelible pencil — sometimes even in blood — was written the letter 'M' to show that they had had morphine.

For the next three hours Lily, and all the other nurses, were run off their feet.

More and more German wounded were now appearing as the Falaise pocket tightened. This time Lily found three very young men, obviously Hitler Youth who had been drafted into the Waffen SS. Despite their injuries they were quite unpleasant.

She had the job of searching their pockets. Her hand closed around something metal and heavy. As she pulled it out, horrified she saw it was a British-type hand grenade. With a scream she threw it away into the nearest hedge.

The German laughed. In three strides one of the stretcher-bearers, she knew him to be of Polish descent, reached him. Geneva Convention or not, the man clouted him so hard that the young Nazi flopped back unconscious.

Another RAMC man raised his rifle at the other two. White-faced they raised their hands.

'Bloody sloppy work by the blokes who should have searched them. You all right, Sister?'

Shaking, Lily pushed her sweating hands down over her apron.

'Yes — thank you.'

'Bloody Nazis — begging your pardon, ma'am.'

Lily smiled, but knew her face must be as white as a sheet as she said, 'That's all right.'

Lily was eventually relieved and off duty by 0200 hours the next day. She got to her bed, took her boots and white nurse's veil off and lay down. She had intended just to rest for a few minutes before she found the energy to freshen up and change properly, but the next time she was aware of anything, it was to find the early summer sunshine pouring through the open flap of the tent doorway onto her face. Lily groaned, turned over, would have tried to sleep on as she wasn't rostered until 14.00 hours, but her bladder wouldn't let her.

She sat up, found her boots, didn't bother to lace them up and trudged out to the latrines — the most hateful part of being in the field, felt by all the girls. Behind a hessian screen was a trench, and across it a board with holes in it. There were no individual partitions. Two girls were already sitting there. Lily joined them. Nobody spoke, they all found it too embarrassing. She'd just finished when Matron came in. That was one of the most frightening things about it — having Matron sit next to you.

Later, Lily set out her folding canvas bath in another screened area, and carried hot water to it.

Carefully, she eased herself in and lay a few minutes, eyes closed, enjoying the luxury of its hot embrace.

She washed her hair vigorously, afraid of catching the lice so many men, especially the

158

Germans, had, and then lathered her body. When she had finished, as she stepped out, the bath collapsed sending a wave of water across the grass.

Dressed, she tackled the bit of washing she had, using the more reliable wash stand. Then, back in her tent, she set up her travelling mirror on her box and began to tidy her face and fixed the starched white veil on her head. They were impracticable, with all the guy ropes, flaps and other obstacles of the tented hospital, but thanks to General Montgomery, who had declared many times that he thought the presence of British nurses comforted and cheered the wounded men, and helped raise morale, they had to wear them. Even Matron had ordered them to put on a little light lipstick — something that would have been a 'crime' in Civvy Street.

'These poor boys have been in battle. They don't want to see you looking exhausted; consider it part of the treatment.'

So, incongruously, she had on her khaki battledress with boots, white veil and lipstick. Lily checked the time. Another twenty minutes before she was due on, and the bugle hadn't sounded, so there was no big rush. She found a much-thumbed copy of *Picture Post*.

Lily was sitting on her bed when a figure

appeared at the entrance. It was a girl from the next-door tent, a bundle of letters in her hand.

'Hon, I've got the post — there are some letters here for you.' She came in and held them out. Lily took them.

'Thanks Cynthia, that's kind of you.'

She put the *Picture Post* aside and looked at the letters. The first was from her mother, the address written in her bold, flowing hand. Shuffling them, the second was from her old school — Cheltenham Ladies. The third and longest had a typed official label, giving her rank, name and BFPO number. It also carried a smudged official-looking rubber stamp, something about a redirection office.

Lily groaned under her breath.

What was wrong now? What army form had she filled in incorrectly? She slipped her nail file under the flap and slit it open. Instead of a letter there was another, smaller envelope. She looked at her name written in ink, in a far from neat hand, and didn't recognize it.

Something started to come over her — conscious that her heart was beating faster.

Could it be — ?

The bugle began its compelling call. There was no way she could not respond to its urgent summons. But there was no way she

160

could leave the letter unopened and concentrate on what she would have to do. Fumbling, she got the nail file under the flap, slit it open, pulled the letter half out, and unfolded the corner.

It was enough.

She read, *My darling Lily* —

Quickly pushing it back into the envelope, she pulled her apron top aside, unbuttoned her battledress pocket, and put it next to her heart, then hurriedly tidied herself up.

She was running for the ambulances with her mind in a turmoil — ecstatic that she had at last heard from him, but frightened now at what he had to say — why he hadn't written before.

Mike was never out of her mind as she started to help with the great tide of broken and bleeding humanity. It was as if he was there, watching everything she did right through to the last boy, who, given his injuries, mercifully died on the table. By the time she got back to her tent the others were fast asleep.

She sat down onto her bed, got out the letter, and looked at it for a long time in the gloom.

Lily had waited so long for this moment, and now she found she had to steel herself to open it. She found her cigarettes, lit one, hand shaking again, and turned up the hurricane lamp slightly.

Eventually she drew the letter out carefully, slowly unfolded it, began to read.

15

He'd given her her night-time medication, including a capsule to make her sleep, or rather, to make sure he, as her carer, got some sleep, then stayed with her until she'd nodded off, before getting his meal, and eating it in the bedroom beside her bed.

Now, as he looked down on her, only her head and face showed, white hair splayed out wildly on the pillow.

Tenderly he smoothed it down with his hand. This really was the only time in the day that they were 'normal' again, the loving, happy couple who had vowed, after the war, never to be parted ever again, not even for a day.

He smiled at that. Of course, it had been impracticable.

Mike's heart ached as he lovingly contemplated her face, now no longer creased up in pain, or fury, or blank with bewilderment, but serene, almost with a trace of a smile. Or was he kidding himself?

He slumped down into the chair beside the bed, found her hand beneath the clothes, held on to it tightly.

He closed his eyes; pretended, let his thoughts go down the years.

So many memories — the children; the holidays; the dances; the dinners; the opera. The first time she had insisted he go because Maria Callas was singing at Covent Garden.

Reluctantly, grumbling, he had gone — and had come away utterly entranced.

Together they had travelled the world, La Scala, Milan, La Fenice, Venice, The Met in New York; even, in the later years, the Sidney Opera House, following their favourites, Geraint Evans, Joan Sutherland, Kiri Te Kanawa, and later Domingo, Carreras and Pavarotti.

He remembered glancing sideways in his seat every time the 'Drinking Song' from *La Traviata* was performed — one of her favourites — watching her eyes light up with pleasure, eyes that now no longer existed except in his memory.

He hung tightly onto her hand, fought back the tears.

And now he would be leaving her, leaving her to while away the rest of her life in some nursing home, among strangers. And he couldn't be sure how she would be treated.

No, he couldn't allow that. When they said they would never be parted again they knew what they had really meant all those years ago.

He realized what he had to do.

For the first time in ages, he longed for a cigarette — a cigarette and a whisky.

And, strangely, as the evening progressed and he had his whisky, though no cigarette, he became happier than he had for a very long time.

★ ★ ★

The slaughter that was the Falaise Pocket was over. The Germans, especially the 12th SS Panzer Division Hitler Jugend had fought with fanatical bravery and it was not until the 16 August that Von Kluge, their commander, ordered a full-scale retreat, a withdrawal finally authorized by the Führer.

Elements of the German 3rd Parachute Division sacrificed themselves to hold open an escape route, but the retreating Germans were shelled non-stop by the Canadians and Americans and attacked incessantly by the Allied Air Force without mercy.

Nevertheless, Mike learnt that a considerable number of the enemy had got away, albeit without their equipment.

He had been one of the RAMC officers who had been called in as the advancing Allied troops overran fields where hundreds of German wounded had been gathered, then abandoned due to the lack of any drugs and doctors.

Now, after days of hectic work, they were once more moving forward in their jeeps and three-tonners, catching up with the armoured regiment. For two days they had passed enormous columns of dirty and dishevelled German prisoners, marching in winding trails of defeat.

And then the scene they were passing through turned into a nightmare of twisted blackened metal and swollen, putrid bodies of men and horses; hundreds of horses, eyes wide and white with terror still in the harness of overturned gun carriages, teeth bared, bodies mutilated by blast and shrapnel.

Tangled piles of grey uniformed corpses lay in sticky pools of dried blood that had flowed along the tarmac, and limbs and viscera hung in the hedges.

And everywhere, papers and photographs were blowing in the gentle breeze. One stuck momentarily to the windscreen, showing a smiling young soldier of the Wehrmacht, with his obviously equally smiling proud parents on either side. Mercifully it flew off.

The scene from hell was sometimes obscured by oily black smoke from still smouldering tyres.

From some of the tanks, shrunken black

bodies, twisted in agony, hung from hatches, or fused together in groups sheltering behind the burnt-out remains of lorries. From their black skulls flashed still white teeth, like a perpetual demonic grin.

They passed a staff car, on its side in a ditch. The officer, a major was slumped on top of a beautiful girl in a silk dress. Her beautiful made-up eyes stared vacantly at the heavens; their baggage lay open and scattered.

Women's dainty undergarments fluttered obscenely in the sunshine.

It was all so quiet, yet it was as if they could still hear the screams, and the very air seemed to throb with explosions that had long since stopped.

As they drove on, the army was already clearing up.

Bulldozers were working, clanking and grinding back and forth as they scooped up the piles of corpses and lumbered with them to great pits dug in the flower-filled meadows, dropping in the rotting, bloody contents.

With a cloud of diesel fumes and the shriek of metal on metal, they reversed away to start the whole process again.

Mike looked at the macabre scene with almost no emotion. His senses had been dulled over the weeks, and his emotion was now reserved for the still living but torn and mutilated men he was dealing with day on day. Without a *soul*, there was nothing there, just putrefying organic matter.

When they reached the regiment, it was to find that it was being rested and held in reserve for forty-eight hours.

Mike left his driver and a couple of the others to pitch their tents and found the adjutant, who looked up from his folding table to say, 'Ah there you are, Doc, good to see you again.'

Mike slumped into a canvas chair.

'Is it true — forty-eight hours?'

The adjutant nodded. 'Yes, could be longer. The Canadian reserves have moved into our position. The big show has wound down now, and the Boche are regrouping on the other side of the Seine — pity really. If we'd kept going I think we could have given them a knock-out blow.'

Mike breathed out. 'Forty-eight hours,' savouring the words.

It seemed like heaven. They hadn't stopped since D-Day. What would he do?

He thought of just the luxury of sleeping all day, but he knew he wouldn't. Perhaps he could commandeer a bike, find a relatively unscathed village, and enjoy a bottle of rustic wine and a bit of bread and cheese — and silence.

Any further dreaming was wiped away by what the adjutant said next.

'Oh, by the way, the post has finally caught up with us. My bloody tailor's bill has arrived. You've got quite a lot apparently — Postie says they're sweet-smelling, you old rogue.'

'Hey — '

Mike ran — past the lines of tanks covered in camouflage among the trees, past the mobile workshops, past the cookhouse and the men's tents, until he came to the single bell tent with the sign outside: Post Office.

He paused, composed himself, ducked and went in.

★   ★   ★

Lily was beside herself. She had read Mike's letter, the one he had written just before D-Day, over and over again, had blurred the ink with tears; had passed from sheer joy to the depths of despair — frightened after what she had witnessed in the last two months knowing that RAMC officers had died in the titanic struggle still going on.

Was he still alive?

And if he was, there was no way of knowing where he might be; the address was from the base camp in England.

She would write immediately. It would find him, but she realized the chances of getting a reply inside weeks was very unlikely — they were, *both*, in the middle of a war.

Still, the Forces Post Office had tracked *her* down — so she would write to his last English BFPO address, and hope it, too, would be forwarded quickly. Otherwise, there was nothing else she could do.

Was there?

Mike was in the RAMC. So were all the surgeons and doctors here, at her hospital.

She would make enquiries first thing in the morning; someone might know him, know where he was.

Still clutching his letter, she turned down the hurricane lamp, and lay on her camp-bed, too excited to sleep. Lily thought of him, of the taste of his shaving soap on his cheek, of the little smile when his mouth curled up, and his boyish look that could become quite steely if he was serious.

But she was deeply, happily, asleep by the time the other girls in her tent woke up, groaning and stretching.

They all giggled and nudged each other at the sight of the letter still clutched in her hand.

★   ★   ★

170

Mike had been overwhelmed by her letters. He read and read them over and over again.

When, eventually, he bound them together with an elastic band, to be enjoyed again later, he took out his cigarettes, sat back, tapping one on his case. He had plenty of time in the next day or so, to reply. Mike thought he would write at least two — hoping one got through — just in case. So much had kept them apart.

He realized that there had always been a part of him that had been with her, even in the darkest of hours. He frowned. Something about the number of her field hospital stuck in his mind. He was sure they were in Normandy. His heart began to beat faster.

On impulse he got to his feet, pushing the cigarette back into his case, and hurried towards the motor transport section and the workshops.

Half an hour later he was on an army Enfield motor bike, wobbling unsteadily against a convoy of trucks full of infantry moving forward. Clouds of dust obscured the road and he was glad the sergeant in the motor pool had insisted he take a pair of goggles. He'd not heard the shouted exhortation to 'Bring the bloody bike back in one piece — sah!'

He almost ran over a military police

sergeant at a crossroads, who stepped forward out of the dust with his hand raised to stop him. Mike brought the bike to a jerking halt, stalling the engine.

The Redcap looked at him suspiciously.

'May I ask what you are doing, sir?'

He realized it must look odd. Officers, especially RAMC officers, didn't usually travel on dispatch riders' bikes. Perhaps the man thought he was deserting or something.

He raised his goggles.

'I'm trying to get to the nearest field dressing station, Sergeant — need to speak to them urgently. Can you point me in the right direction?'

The sergeant was satisfied.

'As far as I'm aware there are two close by, sir, one to the left at the next crossroads, about a quarter of a mile, and another straight on. Do you know which one you want, sir?'

Mike shook his head.

'Not really, but I'll try the nearest.'

In actual fact it didn't matter which one. They would know all the field hospitals in Normandy.

After several kicks, the engine still refused to start, so the sergeant gave him a push. He let in the gear, the engine spluttered, fired, and he was off, leaving the military policeman face down in the road, cursing bloody officers swanning around the country.

Mike drove on, deciding to keep to the main road. Half a mile away he came upon a notice with an arrow: *Dressing Station*.

He turned off, followed its direction all the way down a lane until there it was, a marquee-type tent, with its own white circle and red cross on the roof, numerous small tents, and a fleet of ambulances.

He bumped across some baked mud ridges and swung to a halt by the unit sign for the motor ambulance company.

He cut the engine, got off and pulled the bike onto its stand.

Inside a tent, a warrant officer sat behind a folding table full of records. As soon as he saw Mike he shot to his feet, startled by the appearance of a dishevelled, very dusty unknown RAMC officer, with the outline of the goggles he had raised to his forehead, showing around his eyes like a panda.

'Sir.' He didn't salute, as he did not have his hat on.

Mike nodded, motioned for him to relax.

'Carry on, I can see you're busy. I'm sorry to disturb you, but I need some information urgently.'

The warrant-officer frowned.

'Information about what?'

'Field Hospitals — the nearest one?'

'That would be the 203 — five miles back from here.'

Mike got out one of the letters and checked. It wasn't the same number. He showed the address.

'Any idea where this one is?'

The man shook his head.

'Can't say I do, sir, but there is a whole bunch of them along the Caen-Bayeaux Road, something like five or six I believe.'

Mike pressed his lips together, checked the time, and decided to press on.

'The 203 — easy to find?'

The man nodded.

'Yes, but your luck's in, sir. We have six ambulances going down there now — would you like to go in one?'

Mike shook his head.

'No, thanks. But I'll follow them.'

And he did, the big red cross in the white circle on its back double doors making it easy to see the last one in the convoy despite the continuing clouds of dust.

The 203 was a hive of activity, with ambulances continually arriving and leaving, returning to the dressing stations, or taking the wounded, not to the coast and ships home, but to the newly laid airfields where the injured were being evacuated fast, back to the UK by Dakota transport aircraft.

Although he was expecting it, it still came as a shock to see nurses in their large white caps, albeit worn with battledress. The sight brought him up with a start. He hadn't seen nurses since he'd left Lily. For one heart-stopping moment he even thought he caught a glimpse of her, then got a grip of himself. But he still couldn't take his eyes off every nurse that came his way.

Eventually he found his way to the tent of the CO of the hospital, a lieutenant colonel, and presented himself.

The CO stood up, leaned forward across his desk and proffered his hand. As they shook, he said, 'Gibson, eh? You're up the sharp end with the Guards Division, aren't you? We've seen some of your handiwork come through here, very good indeed.'

For the next ten minutes Mike had to bear with the CO, listening as the latter discussed how the evacuation system was working, and the tricks they were picking up as they went along.

Mike eventually began to get impatient. Perhaps it showed, for the CO suddenly said, 'So what brings you here?'

He explained that he was looking for one field hospital in particular.

The CO sat back, gave a knowing grin. 'It's a nurse, isn't it?'

Mike, feeling his face redden, blurted out, 'Yes, sir. We were together for a while before being separated prior to D-Day. I've just had word she's with a field hospital over here. I'm trying to track her down. You see, we are going to be married after the war's ended — we're engaged.'

Where that came from he had no idea, but it left him feeling light-headed, hearing the unspoken thoughts said aloud for the first time. And the little lie should surely help?

He pulled out the envelope.

The CO winced in mock horror.

'Better watch out for Matron when you do find her. Now, let's see that address.'

Mike handed it over.

Immediately the CO nodded.

'Ah, yes, they're here.'

As Mike's heart leapt he turned to a filing cabinet, yanked open a drawer, and thumbed through some folders. Eventually he pulled one out.

Mike clearly saw the title: *War Office, Order of Battle/Medical Units. North west Europe.*

He turned the pages until near the back he stopped, ran a finger down a list.

'Here we are. It's deployed in Sector five

off the Caen-Bayeaux road.'

He got up, went to the map stuck on the side of a metal cupboard.

Mike joined him as the CO traced his finger along the road leading out of Bayeaux towards Caen, then stopped and tapped it lightly on one spot.

'There, that's where they are.'

Mike moved in closer, took in the detail, jotted down some notes on the back of the envelope.

He could hardly believe it. Lily was there, only eighteen to twenty kilometres away.

'I should be able to reach there before nightfall.'

The CO straightened up.

'Better make sure you do. Some people are still a bit trigger-happy at night, especially the French. Had a few casualties in already.'

The CO could see the young fellow before him was itching to be on his way, and he knew that when young love called, nothing else mattered. He stuck out his hand.

'Well, best of luck — to you both.'

Mike shook it firmly.

'Thank you, sir.'

He stood back and saluted.

When he'd gone, the CO sat back down and mused. It had been a bit like that for him and Rosemary back in 1918. She and her parents had come down to Dover, where they had married on a 'Forty-Eight', before he'd gone back to his unit. Even there, in England, they'd heard the rumble of the guns in Flanders, carrying all the way across the Channel.

Astride the bike, feet on the ground, Mike unscrewed the cap on the petrol tank, and juggled the machine from side to side. The petrol sloshed around inside the tank, but it sounded pretty empty.

After a few kicks on the starter lever, the engine fired. He motored over to the RASC fuel point, and managed to persuade a corporal to fill him up.

Back at the main road in the early evening sun, he began to drive faster, swerving in and out of convoys and the columns of marching men.

He could hardly dare to believe he would see her soon. Doubts racked his mind — she'd been moved since she had written; she'd fallen ill; had been sent home;

She'd been *killed*.

Although he knew that was fanciful, being stupid, the fact remained; nurses had died on active service, especially in torpedoed troop-ships, and in the Far East with the barbarous Japanese. But he knew the Germans were very respectful of the red cross signs.

But anything could have happened. Traffic accidents happened all the time.

All this went through his mind as he drove hard, back along the way that he had come with the Guards. Back down the road that had cost so many lives.

16

Lily woke up with a start; sat up, looking around, knew she was happy.

Then it all came back with a rush. Her hand flew to her breast pocket, it was empty. She had a moment of panic, wondering if she'd imagined the whole thing, then found it in the bed.

Lily could have screamed out loud with happiness. Instead, she scrambled to get ready, having overslept quite badly. Although they were no longer under the great pressure of the last few weeks, Matron, to say nothing of the nurse she was due to relieve, would not be best pleased. Even so, she took time to read it once again before rolling her apron aside and pushing it into her breast pocket.

Running, with her hand on her white cap, she made it just in time, ducking in through the open flap of the tent.

Jenny, the girl she was relieving, took her through the change-over notes.

'Well, that's it, pretty quiet, thank God. Oh, have you heard? We're moving.'

Lily looked at her.

'What do you mean?'

Jenny collected her bits and pieces and paused in the doorway.

'Now the front line has moved further away, we're being relocated — somewhere much nearer. It's going to happen all the time until the war is over.'

Horrified, Lily asked, 'Do you know where?'

The girl shrugged. 'No. We'll only know when we get there. Anyway, doesn't make any difference, does it?'

With that she was gone.

Lily leaned on a trolley, suddenly anxious. They'd only just got in touch, and now *this*.

As she checked her instrument and drug lists, Lily's happy mood faltered.

Would it be the start of another period of no contact? It didn't bear thinking about.

As soon as she got a quiet moment, she resolved to start a letter to him — even at the risk of being caught by Sister, or worse, Matron.

Eight hours later, with a letter for Mike she had penned inside the pages of a War Office large record pad, thanks to the lull in the heavy fighting, she stepped out into the warm evening air, heavy with the smell of freshly cut hay.

She pulled off her nurse's cap, shook out her hair, uncaring if anybody had a go at her, and walked between the lines of tents, eager to get to the post tent.

Somewhere, somebody was playing records, the light tenor voice carrying in the still evening air telling of a nightingale singing in Berkeley Square. She turned a corner, and became aware of a figure standing there, face in the shadows.

In uniform.

Very dusty and dishevelled.

There was something familiar about him.

She slowed, frowning.

Strangely, he didn't move, just stood there, watching her.

Lily faltered and stopped.

It was only then that the figure moved forward into the evening sunlight.

For several seconds she thought she hadn't woken up — that she was dreaming. She was still in her 'dream' when the figure spoke.

'Lily.'

She swallowed, unable to believe it.

'It *is* you, isn't it, Mike?'

He nodded. 'Yes.'

They came closer, searched each other's face, hardly able to believe what was happening.

When they did, it was instant — rushing forward into each other's arms, Lily hanging on tight as he swung her round and round before setting her down. He put one hand behind her head, lips pressed into her sweet-smelling hair, the other around her waist, Lily with her head pressed hard against his chest, arm wrapped tightly around him, eyes closed.

They stayed like that for some time, before tenderly they found each other's lips.

When they reluctantly drew apart, enough to breathe in the warmth of each other's breath, she whispered, 'I thought I'd never see you again.' She felt tears in her eyes.

Mike murmured, 'I was frightened I'd lost you.'

She pulled away, dabbed at each eye in turn with the base of her thumb.

'Darling, where are you? I mean, where have you come from?'

Mike smiled.

'Would you believe it, I'm just up the road — about twenty kilometres or so? I borrowed a motor bike.'

Still overcome with emotion, she chuckled nervously.

'Will you get into trouble?'

Mike shrugged. 'I don't care.'

She sniffed, found her handkerchief.

'When do you have to go back?'

Reluctantly he said, 'Tomorrow.'

They said nothing until Mike whispered,

'Can you get away — at least for just a while?'

Lily looked up at him. 'I'm off duty for the rest of the night. We could go off somewhere — ?'

He nodded. 'Wonderful.'

Lily became businesslike.

'Stay here. I'll go and get us some food and something to drink.'

As she turned away, he grabbed her roughly, drew her back to him, brought his mouth down hard around hers. They kissed, fiercely, and then she pushed him off.

There was a glint in her eye.

'Wait.'

She walked away.

Mike watched her until she was out of sight, full of irrational fear. He should never have let her go.

Lily did come back, breathless, carrying a wicker supply basket which he quickly took from her.

In the field next door, away from the ack-ack guns, they took a handle each of the basket as they walked through the new mown hay, not talking.

It was twilight and, apart from the drone of a far off aircraft, that ironically seemed to intensify the silence, all that could be heard was the sound of insects, and distant birds — skylarks.

Not a sound of war.

They came to a small stream and a grassy bank dotted with daises and buttercups.

Anxiously, Lily looked around.

'Be careful, the Germans have left a lot of mines. We've had a lot of casualties from the back areas — including children.'

In the gloom he could see no sign of disturbed earth, or notices that said '*Achtung Minen.*'

'Seems all right. Stay here though.'

With that he set down the basket and walked carefully around, especially near the river-bank.

Lily called, 'Do be careful.'

Eventually he came back. 'It's fine, come on.'

They picked up the basket, found a nice area of short grass.

She spread the tablecloth, set out the food, then sat down, legs to one side.

Mike sat opposite, watched as she undid a thermos, poured some hot tea, handing him the Bakelite cup.

'Thank you.'

He let his fingers touch hers. She smiled, blew a kiss.

He tucked in to slices of spam and bread, cheese, biscuits and apples.

She nibbled, but most of the time she just

watched him, still frightened it was all some sort of hallucination.

He looked up, caught her, and grinned sheepishly.

'Sorry, but I haven't eaten since this morning.'

It wasn't his eating she was noticing. Somehow he'd subtly changed.

Mike still looked the same, albeit thinner, harder, but there was something else . . .

Then she realized what it was. He had that air about him that she'd grown used to seeing in the damaged young men who had passed through her hands; young men who had been exposed to war in all its obscenity; who had in a few short weeks aged in a way that others never did in a lifetime.

And Mike had obviously been there, at the front line.

Now, he had that same manner, of a young man with young ways and movements, but a maturity that wasn't there before; a paradox born of the awful times they were living through.

It stirred an immediacy in her. Putting the remains of the meal aside, she moved onto the tablecloth, on her side, leaning on her elbow, hand supporting her head, and looked up at him. Her other arm was draped over the curve of her hip.

There could be no mistaking her desire.

Mike eased across to her, settling alongside. Slowly, gently he brought his face close to hers, held it there for a second.

When he moved again and brought his lips to hers, she closed her eyes.

It began gently, lovingly, but became firmer, wilder.

Lily rolled onto her back as he pressed down on her. She could feel his hardness, and the urgency exploded in her head.

When it was over they lay, with him still inside her, reluctant to part.

Eventually, nature had its way and she felt him leave.

Mike fell to her side. They said nothing, just held hands, stayed like that until Lily cuddled up against him. He wrapped an arm around and kissed her again, burying his face in her hair.

The sun had long set below the wheat sheafs on the far side of the river-bank when they made love a second time.

He kissed her all over her face and then went down onto her neck. Giggling, she struggled to get away, head turning from side to side, hitting him ineffectually on his arm, but he held her firmly.

When he went from her neck, down onto her breast, she suddenly ceased struggling —

They stayed on the river-bank all night, talking, cuddling, lying on their backs, smoking and looking up at the stars.

Lily pointed up at the shimmering white Milky Way.

'Just think of all the things — the moments in history — they've seen, and will see, long after we've all gone, back to dust.'

Mike grinned.

'They can't see.'

She squeezed his hand.

'How do you know?'

He squeezed back, but said nothing. It was a magical night, perhaps she was right.

Towards dawn they made love for the last time, then ran hand in hand into the freezing cold stream, splashing each other for only a short time, then he helped her back out onto the bank.

He used the tablecloth to help dry her, then himself.

Dressed, they looked around the little grassy bank, at the still closed-up daisies, and up at the willow trees and heard the first twittering of the skylarks high above them.

Lily slipped her arm through his.

'I shall remember this place as long as I live.'

Mike agreed.

'Maybe we can come back here again, after the war.'

She squeezed his arm.

'I'd like that.'

They paused once more as they got to the meadow, looked back yet again. She whispered, 'I don't want to leave — I don't want you to leave.'

He said nothing — he couldn't.

As they walked across the field, the top of the hospital tents came into view, and the sound of engines revving, voices shouting.

It was back to reality, back to the war. She looked at her watch.

'I'm due on in a couple of hours.'

He winced. 'I'm sorry, you'll be tired.'

She gave him a nudge.

'And whose fault is that?'

He grinned. 'Mine.'

She nodded. 'Yours. And don't you worry, I'll breeze through my shift, I've never felt better in all my life.'

Several nurses looked at them as they wandered through the camp even though they were not touching. Some giggled and shot him sideways glances.

Out of the corner of her mouth she murmured, 'You've turned a few heads.'

His bike was still where he had left it. Conscious of all the people around them, and the fear of Matron on her rounds at this time of day, they stood apart as she said, 'I don't want you to go.'

Mike replied, 'I don't want to go.'

'Then stay here.'

Mike looked down at his feet.

'You know I can't. And if I get court-martialled it will be a long time before we can see each other again.'

Lily scowled.

'I hate this war.'

Gently, he reminded her, 'It brought us together.'

Silently they stood for several seconds before he said, 'Well, I'd better be going.'

He slung his leg over the bike, switched on the petrol.

She moved nearer.

'Oh, God, Mike, you will be careful, won't you?'

He said, 'Of course. I'm a doctor, don't forget — I'm not in the tanks or the poor bloody infantry.'

She knew he was being disingenuous. He could be shelled, or bombed like anybody else, even taken prisoner. But she knew there was no point in pressing it.

Instead she said, 'At least we are in contact now.'

Mike smiled up at her.

'We are, aren't we?'

There was a pause, which he broke by pushing the machine off its stand and sitting astride it.

Anxiously, she said, 'Mike, we will be able to meet again — soon — won't we?'

He tried to sound optimistic, though he knew it was highly unlikely.

'As soon as I get any leave, or a stand down, I'll find you.'

She looked at him imploringly.

'That's a promise?'

He grinned, and tried to make a joke of it.

'No, it's a threat.'

He kicked down on the starter lever. It took three goes before the engine fired up. He pulled in the clutch lever, engaged first with the foot lever, and took another long look at her.

Suddenly, without caring about Matron, about anyone — they could all go to hell — she leant forward and kissed him on the cheek.

With a roar he wobbled away.

When he reached a corner at the end of a row of tents, he stopped, put a foot down, turned and looked back at her.

They stared at each other for some time. She almost convinced herself that he couldn't go on, that he would turn back.

But then, quite simply, he was gone.

Lily was still there when some of her friends came past.

'Hello, Hon, where have you been?'

She turned, tears streaming down her face.

'Heaven.'

17

The morning dawned bright, the sun streaming in from a crack in the curtains onto the flowered paper on the end wall of the bedroom. But it was the birds singing outside his open window that had woken him up.

Mike lay for some time, contemplating the decision he had come to, before stretching out a hand and turning on the radio.

When it came, the news was full of wars — or armed conflicts as many of them were now called. It was all so depressing, and familiar. Would the world never learn? It was not for his generation to worry about, but he feared for his grandchildren, for the youth of the day.

Slowly he sat up, swivelled around and set his feet gently down onto the floor. Since the cancer had taken hold, his frailty was markedly more apparent. It was one of the reasons for his haste now. Every passing week was marked by a decline in his strength. In another month he would not be able to do what he intended, would not have the strength required.

He looked across at her bed. She was still asleep thanks to the pills.

Well, this was it, this was the day. It had taken some organizing, but he'd managed it.

The easiest and the most obvious place to have gone back to, the place where they had first become as one, no longer existed.

The wartime camp had long been torn down — they'd passed it once twenty years ago. A Tesco store and a housing estate now occupied the site.

That left only one other option: a special place. A place they said they would remember as long as they lived . . . *lived*.

The agency nurse had arrived yesterday. They were off to France, to Normandy, only this time nobody would be shooting at them.

Despite all their promises, they'd never been back, except passing through quickly on their way to somewhere else, usually down south, to the Mediterranean coast with a car full of noisy children.

Until now.

★ ★ ★

It had been a wet, miserable autumn and now it was a long, bitter winter. Far from the war being over by Christmas, as was the talk after Falaise, the Germans had regrouped,

194

and fought like tigers. There had followed one hard battle after another, Bruges, Brussels, Antwerp and Nijmegen. The Guards battalion to which he was attached had been part of the dash to relieve the 6th Airborne at Arnhem, that had failed so disastrously.

Now they were bogged down on the banks of the Lower Rhine. They were at the gates of the enemy. Mike struggled through the mud and ice to his tent, stayed fully clothed except for his boots which he swapped for an extra pair of thick wool socks before getting into his sleeping bag.

To supplement the dim light of the hurricane lamp hanging from a roof support, he lit a candle and put it onto the ammo box that served as his bedside table.

Fumbling with the cold, he got out his fountain pen and picked up his writing pad. Normally he would have written the day before, but he had been unexpectedly busy.

Suddenly, in front of their sector, in the middle of the night, small boats had appeared out of the blackness of the River Rhine.

The forward picket lines had opened fire before the screams of 'We are Dutch' were finally heard by an officer who ordered a cease-fire. The boats were full of families, who were starving to death. Tragically, a girl aged twelve and two men had been killed in the shooting.

He had been shaken awake by an orderly with a torch, scrambling around in the freezing gloom to get his boots on.

When he got to the treatment tent, it was to be confronted by a shivering, gaunt crowd of white-faced men and women begging for food.

He ordered as many blankets as possible to be found and given to them, and arranged for the catering corps kitchens to make a lot of hot soup to be sent forward to them, conscious that in their undernourished state, especially the children, a sudden intake of anything heavier could lead to trouble.

He set in motion their evacuation, spending all the next day getting the transport sorted out and permission for civilians to be sent down the line. And there had still been his usual duties, caring for trench feet, diarrhoea and the odd casualty from sniper or shellfire.

So it was only now that he had the time to write to her. By the flickering light of the candle he began:

My Darling Lily
I hope you are managing to keep warm
in this appalling weather. Nothing much

to report here other than the Dutch people are suffering terribly. Unless something happens soon, they will start dying in their hundreds from starvation and cold. Treated some civilians, including children. Must have seen everything this accursed war has to offer.

He wondered if the censor would delete that, but surely it was widely known, and in any case, of no strategic importance to the enemy who knew it already.

I long to see you again, to hold you in my arms. When will this bloody war end? The night we spent together by the river will remain with me until the day I die.
   You will marry me, Lily, as soon as we can, won't you? I don't want to delay a second more than we have to, to make you my wife.

He knew he was rambling a bit, but it was too cold to focus properly, and he was so very tired.

Darling, I'm so sleepy. Forgive me, but I'll sign off now. Will write again soon.
   I love you, I love you.
   I pray for the day when we can be

together — never to be parted, ever again.
Love you,
Mike

He had no way of knowing that this 'accursed war' had, indeed, one more horror to offer. One that the most corrupt imagination of Hell could ever have conceived.

And it was on this earth.

* * *

Lily's hospital was now north west of Antwerp in the grounds of an estate, the lines of tents linked by duckboards placed on the churned muddy earth that had once been the formal gardens. Nearby was an airfield from which a constant stream of Dakotas flew the wounded back to England.

Her hospital had now been reconfigured as an urgent surgical centre for those who desperately needed treatment before they could even be evacuated — if ever.

Lily was having a typical day, assisting the surgeons as they cleared the blood and pus from an abdominal wound. Bits of the man's small intestine were protruding from his body.

Once that was done, the next case involved

the amputation of a gangrenous arm. The patient had been on oxygen for twelve hours before the decision was taken to remove it.

After him came a leg amputation. Later, she treated a Canadian with septicaemia, who had been expected to die for days. Lily fixed him up with yet another blood transfusion, this time with him chatting pleasantly as opposed to the last time when his mind had been wandering.

She was back in theatre for a newly arrived casualty who had been hit by pieces of shrapnel. The soldier, a major, had already had his left arm amputated and both his eyes removed by a forward surgical team, but the sucking wound in his chest needed more specialist care.

An hour later, the man who had had his gangrenous arm amputated began to show signs of distress. His pulse had become unsteady and weak. He died as he was given another large injection of the penicillin. Wonder drug or not, it could not always work miracles.

Lily was with the major when he came round from the anaesthetic. He started struggling, pulling at the drip, babbling incoherently, thrashing around so much that she had to call others to help her restrain him. Every now and then he let out a great scream that could be heard all over the wards.

One of the surgeons gave him a quarter of a grain of morphine. Within fifteen minutes he had calmed down, and spoke in a gravelly voice.

'Tell me the truth, the *truth* now, what's left of me? Have I lost my legs?'

She reassured him. 'No, of course not.'

Fortunately he didn't ask about anything else, and soon lapsed into incoherence again. She tried to take his pulse — but it was imperceptible. Late in the evening he suddenly rose up, vomited a stream of blood and mucus, rolled to one side as she reached him, and died in her arms.

That night two more died on her shift, one with crushed urethras who had died in agony unable to pass urine and another with gas gangrene that had been detected as soon as they had removed the bloody bandages. It was to be expected, as they were a unit dedicated to those who were not expected to live.

Eventually relieved of duty, back in her tent, she pulled off her cap, sank down into a chair, and cried. It was more exhaustion than anything. She would have to go through it all again tomorrow, and the day after, and the day after that *ad nauseam* until it was all over.

She gained control of herself before

anybody could see her, found her handkerchief and blew her nose. It would never do for Matron to hear about it, though from time to time recently there had been lapses in her stern visage. It would appear that, after all, there was a human heart deep beneath that stiffly starched white apron.

Like she did every night, when she'd finished her toilet and got into bed, Lily fished out his latest letter.

After she read it she gave it a kiss, then put it under her pillow, before turning down the wick and extinguishing her bedside lamp.

In the dark she thought of Mike. His letters in the last few months had become darker. It worried her that he was beginning to suffer from depression.

It was 15 December. Perhaps with the lull in fighting, they might be able to meet over the Christmas period, although the cold, snowy weather was going to make that difficult, even if he could get away, but it would cheer him up to write and tell him of her proposal.

Lily went to sleep encouraged by the thought. It was next day that rumours began to circulate about a huge German offensive — could that be true? They were already nearly beaten, surely?

In the next few days a few facts mixed with

more rumours mushroomed out of all proportion. They had broken through in the Ardennes, a hilly, forested area where they had struck in 1940, and were well on their way to splitting the Allies in two and reaching Antwerp. The hospital was on standby to move at very short notice.

Shocked, Lily and the rest of the nurses carried on with their duties, breaking off when possible to gather around the wireless sets that were giving out bulletins.

Lily realized that not only was her dream of seeing Mike over Christmas in ruins, but that if the Germans succeeded, he would be cut off from her, possibly in even greater peril. Fortunately, the pressing nature of her work kept her mind from dwelling on the awful prospect.

Off duty, she hastily scribbled a short letter to him, put it into the postbag without any hope that it would get to him in the near future.

The Battle of the Bulge, as somebody had called it, was still going on, and now it was snowing badly again. No aircraft were flying, no casualties being evacuated.

Lily, like all of them, felt utterly dejected. They had so taken it for granted that the war was heading to a finish, sooner rather than later. And now this. Not only was the end seemingly further away than ever, there was even a chance that a disaster was about to occur.

But all she could think of was Mike, and his safety.

18

The hotel was in Caen, a small *pension* really, run by one family. They understood the problem and couldn't have been more helpful, even though he'd brought his own nurse with him.

Thanks to her medication, Lily sat at the breakfast table needing only a little help with her feeding. Her eyes kept darting about, taking in the shiny copper kettles and pans with which the room was decorated.

Mike ate quickly; he had a full morning planned, starting with the arrival of a hired car and driver. He left Lily with the nurse when the Citroën came for him.

He told the driver what he wanted. Fortunately the man was local and although he had no idea of the exact location of the place, they were soon in the general area.

They drove down the main road and turned off to the right. This time there was no wreckage, no ruined, roofless houses, abandoned blackened tanks, dead cows and the all-pervading smell of death. Only new roads, bewildering rows of neat homes, new supermarkets, rebuilt churches and everywhere expansion. So much of the countryside had been built over.

He suddenly tapped the dashboard. 'Slow down.'

They were going past a little round-turreted church. Half of the stones were newer — looking, but the tiles on the roof were a modern uniform red colour. The last time he'd seen it was with the roof blown off and the walls reduced to rubble.

But he recognized it, because he had stopped his motor bike outside and asked directions from a military policeman as he tried to find her hospital.

It was a good start.

But an hour later they were no nearer to his goal, indeed he had started to despair.

They stopped for a coffee and a small, fiery calvados, which he knew he shouldn't be having, but he needed it. And besides — what the hell? So it would shorten his life?

He chuckled as they spread out the maps on the counter, and his driver entered into a torrent of French with the proprietor, with much stabbing of fingers on the paper.

'Well?'

His driver shrugged his shoulders in only the way the French can.

'He says he has lived here for thirty years and doesn't know anything about the war. The only thing he can suggest is that you go to the farmhouse down the end of the cul-de-sac.' He pointed beyond their parked car. 'The family that own it have done so for a hundred years — they might know more.'

Mike nodded at the proprietor.

'*Merci, monsieur.*'

He felt better after the calvados. The driver saw him into the car, slamming the door and getting in behind the wheel.

The road down to the farm started off quite well, but for the last mile or so it descended into potholes that shook up his weakened body and he winced with pain.

They turned in front of a typical Normandy farm building, with rusty agricultural machinery sheltering a few ground-pecking hens. A dog raised its head from the flagstones by the door, then stood up and barked.

His driver hesitated to get out, but the front door opened and a woman emerged and silenced it, standing, waiting, with arms crossed. The driver got out and walked over to her.

Mike watched as they talked animatedly, the driver turning to point at him.

Suddenly the woman started towards the car, the driver following behind. The woman appeared at his window, which he had lowered.

Relieved, he could see she was smiling, and in the torrent of French he caught the word 'Tommy'.

The driver translated.

'She says you are very welcome to come inside — to speak to her grandfather who lived here in the war. You are very welcome because you were a Tommy, and when I explained that you were also a doctor she was quite excited.'

Down a dark, dingy corridor with a load of antlers on a wall they entered into a family room with a range stove at one end, a selection of easy chairs and a table. Everywhere the smell of cooking with garlic pervaded. In a high-winged chair was a man roughly of his own age, smoking a blackened pipe who turned out to have a good command of English.

He grinned, showing yellow, twisted teeth.

'It is always a pleasure to meet people from those days.'

After interruptions from his granddaughter, who bustled off to make coffee, they started reminiscing about 1944.

It turned out that the old boy had been in the Resistance, and remembered vividly receiving the radio messages from London.

He cackled *'Ici Londres, ici Londres — Bercent mon coeur d'une langueur.'*

He waved his pipe in the air.

'We knew then, you see, we knew it was coming, the invasion.'

It was apparent that the fellow enjoyed meeting anyone from the past. It quite animated him according to his granddaughter.

With another cup of coffee, and an even larger glass of calvados, Mike let him chatter on, before he said eventually, 'I'm looking for the site of a British field hospital — it was around here somewhere.'

The pipe, which had taken the opportunity to find its way back to the yellowy teeth, was abruptly removed.

'*Mon Dieu*, there were so many of them. I believe you English had a name — '

Mike cut in, 'Harley Street.'

'Yes, yes, that was it. I knew them all.'

'You did?'

The Frenchman took a sip of calvados.

'Oh yes, there were three over the other side of the main road, and two this side, one on our land.'

Excited, Mike leaned forward.

'You don't by any chance have a stream running through your farm?'

'Yes, we do.' It was the granddaughter who had replied.

'And was one of the hospitals near it?'

The pipe was pointed at him. 'Yes. Were you one of the doctors?'

Happily Mike nodded, keeping it simple. 'Oh yes. And my wife was one of the nurses.'

'Is she dead?'

The question shocked him. For a few seconds he didn't answer, and then heard himself say, 'Yes.'

Because it was true.

★ ★ ★

It was Christmas Eve, 1944.

He stood in the snow, with a few flakes still slowly coming down, gathered with the others around a brazier made from a used oil drum somebody had found, stamping their feet and holding their woollen-gloved hands out above the flames.

The padre had conducted a service with carols, and now they were singing more sentimental stuff.

A Welsh Guardsman was crooning the Bing Crosby number 'White Christmas'.

Everybody was quiet, thinking of home.

Mike stared into the glowing depths, seeing shapes like he had as a child, before closing his eyes, imagining he was with Lily, that they were married, and at home, and the war was over: that he was a practitioner in a country town, perhaps somewhere in the Cotswolds, or Olney in Buckinghamshire where his best friend at the hospital had come from and with whom he had often stayed.

At least the great fear of the last few days, of her being in the path of the German offensive, had passed.

Whilst it was still dangerous, it looked as though the Yanks had finally stemmed the flow. Word was going around that the 101st Airborne's heroic holding of Bastoigne had put a spanner in Hitler's great plan.

But it had shocked and then depressed everybody's spirits. There seemed to be no end to the Germans' strength and fighting spirit. They were never going to give up easily.

Eventually he moved away, glad to snuggle into his new sleeping bag, still fully dressed but now at least without his greatcoat, which he put over the top.

He could still hear somebody singing, '*Just the way you looked tonight*'.

Lily was in his mind as he slowly drifted off to sleep.

It was duty as normal for her. She was on the ward when a little group of nurses, in full uniform of grey dresses, scarlet cloaks — still flecked with snowflakes — and white veils, carrying a festive lamp, came in singing carols.

Even in their critical condition, the men, at least those who were conscious, stirred and listened.

A tear flowed from a burly sergeant-major's eye as he remembered carol singing with his two boys, followed by snowball fights. His legs now ended just above the knees.

The nurses stayed for just five minutes before moving on to the next ward. She gave a little wave to one of her friends as they went.

It was the same friend who with another, had persuaded her to go to Brussels last October. She had felt guilty, but had been told quite definitely that there was no way she could go up to the front to see him. So —

But it had in the beginning felt terribly wrong. As it turned out, the seventy-two-hour pass to the newly liberated city had been a wonderful experience, and served to refresh them all from the daily horror they had been pitched into since Normandy.

To begin with, they were housed in a real brick and stone building, in fact a luxury hotel that had been commandeered as an officers' mess — with great chandeliers in the entrance hall, and a marble floor and magnificent stairways.

In the rooms there were wardrobes with coat hangers, but above all, the luxury of running water, and the ability to have a soak in hot water in a proper bath. Outside, the Belgians were unconstrained in their welcome, and the shops were full of goods. They found that they could get khaki skirts, tailored ones, made in best barathea, which was marvellous after the baggy battledress trousers.

The only thing she had trouble with was the socializing in the officers' mess, in the grand ballroom of the hotel.

The girls had pleaded, 'Oh come on, Lily, the lads have been through hell. It's our duty, just like nursing, to cheer them up.'

Lily was far from convinced, but tagged along. The dancing was not to a wind-up gramophone but a three-piece band, and there were oceans of champagne. In fact, in that autumn in liberated Europe there was more champagne available than clean water — or so it seemed.

The officers competed to dance with them, but Lily found that most of them just wanted to talk about their wives and girlfriends back home, show her photographs. Others just wanted to feel normal, talking to a woman, flirting, having a good time.

On the way back, at the end of their 'seventy-two', as they bounced around in a three-tonner, they laughed and joked about their time in Brussels, and that they would remember it for ever. As they turned into the hospital camp somebody moaned, 'My God, it's back to curfews again.'

Nurses in military, and civilian hospitals were always subject to curfew. The freedom had been fantastic.

But, for Lily, any longer would have seemed a betrayal of Mike.

As the ward fell silent again Lily got on with her work. At least the German offensive was now apparently no longer the threat it had been, and where Mike was, seemed quiet. Assuming he was where she thought he was.

Perhaps the New Year would bring fresh hope, that it would all end in 1945.

19

Mike frowned out of the car window. They had passed where the man had said the hospital had stood on their land, and had come across a large distribution warehouse. Nowhere was recognizable.

The car got to the end of the tarmac road and faced a rusty chain-linked fence, with beyond a wild hedge of brambles. Rubbish and twisted strips of packing, bottles, cans and old oil drums lay everywhere.

Disappointed, the driver began turning into the parking area by the access ports of the building. Articulated lorries were being loaded by forklift trucks.

It was only when he was right alongside the fence, and a gap appeared in the hedge, that he had a glimpse beyond of a meadow, with, in the distance, a new high-speed rail line.

Suddenly he jerked up.

'Stop. Stop the car.'

He made the driver get him out, and help him through the broken fence, forcing his way past the brambles that tore at his coat, then help him down a muddy ditch and up the other side.

And there it was: the same bank of the stream that they had spent the night together so long ago, in the summer of '44, in the midst of a momentous time in history.

Same, but not the same.

The stream was brown, and seemed far smaller, as did the whole area. An upturned shopping trolley rusted in the water, and plastic bottles bobbed and nudged each other in the foaming shallows.

In the long grass he could see discarded hypodermic needles, it was a place obviously used by drug addicts.

The field through which they had come to reach it was now the large warehouse, its side, with scrapped machinery of some sort stacked beside it, threw a dark shadow over the area.

And in the distance was the new railway and the roar of the trains passing along it.

It was heart-breaking. He should never have come. The old adage was right — never go back. Memories in the mind should remain in the mind.

Sadly he turned away.

It was then that he saw that it was easier to get where they were standing by going around the building in the car. The fence was missing. This way he could drive the car right up to where he was, albeit with a bump over the shallow ditch.

That tipped the balance for him. He had already realized that the way they had come was too difficult to manage on his own, let alone with her, and in the dark. He would have had to have had help and that would have been impossible. This way, he could drive the car right up to where he was standing.

It made his mind up.

He'd come too far not to go on and, though the area had changed for the worse, so had his cancer.

He'd been reminded by the old farmer that the code warning of the imminence of D-Day had been the line from Paul Verlaine's poem:

Bercent mon coeur d'une langueur.

And somewhere he remembered a line from that same poem that translated into the wounded heart. That's what he had, a wounded heart.

It was time to heal it — for ever.

★   ★   ★

The unremitting cold weather of January lasted into February, but the next momentous step towards the end of the war was already being planned, and the build up of men and *matériel* was seen daily. Enormous

216

American-made trucks towing trailers with Churchill tanks, and lorries with mounted 40mm Bofors anti-aircraft guns poured into their sector, together with extra battalions of infantry.

By early March the thaw had at last set in; the trees dripping melted water. The remaining snow left on the branches reminded Mike of twisted used bandages. Despite the mud the build-up continued.

By 15 March everybody was being briefed on the last great battle of the war in the west — the crossing of the Rhine.

Mike went to a meeting about the medical evacuation, and to liaise with the airborne medics who were being deployed as part of the largest airborne assault of the war — a force of 22,000 to be dropped immediately behind the German lines across the Rhine. Eighty thousand British and Canadian troops would assault a twenty mile stretch of the river.

On 16 March, a massive smoke-screen hid the arrival of thirty-six navy landing-craft and an engineering battalion with bridge pontoons.

He wrote a cheerful note to Lily on the eighteenth, wondering after he had sent it, if he hadn't been too cheerful. Lily was nobody's fool. He knew she had hinted several times that she was worried about him being 'gloomy' as she put it.

But the sight of the landing-craft had sent a spasm of fear through him. He remembered nearly ten months previously, and the slaughter on the beaches of Normandy. Would it happen again, only worse?

He didn't have to wait long to find out.

In the late afternoon of the 23 March, a massive artillery barrage opened up, and went on for hours, before, at 2100 hours the spearhead units of the 79th Armoured Division, driving Buffalo armoured amphibious personnel carriers made for the river.

There was only light resistance and by dawn the troops were securing the opposite banks as the engineers rushed to build their bridges.

Then came the thunderous roar of aircraft. The heavy drone was deafening and went on for some time as wave after wave of bombers and gliders went past overhead. The sky darkened, and seemed to be full of aircraft as far as the eye could see. They watched in awe, standing on the bonnet of the jeep.

Eventually the time came for Mike and his unit to join the massive traffic jam as everybody headed for the Rhine, waved forward by military police, the Redcaps, with signal batons.

They crossed the river hours later, on the

long pontoon bridge the engineers had constructed so amazingly quickly. It was just short of a mile in length.

By then resistance had stiffened — as always with the Germans.

Forward units came up against machine-gun and mortar nests of the German 1st Parachute Army.

Soon Mike was busy with the usual harvest of the broken and smashed bodies of men at the beginning of their adult life — clamping, compressing, suturing, transfusing blood and plasma, injecting penicillin.

Later, they learned that the American General Patton's Third Army tanks had seized a railway bridge at Remegen on the 7 March, almost without casualties. It had been deliberately kept from them in case it sapped their will to be aggressive.

★　★　★

Lily and her hospital heard of the crossing through the BBC radio broadcasts. As they gathered around the sets, cheering — unless Matron was in the vicinity — her anxiety level soared. Where was Mike in all this?

She had long since realized that he was in a far more forward position than he had led her to believe.

Soon afterwards they were informed that the hospital was on the move again. Reports were coming in that the Allied advance was gathering pace. Nobody knew where they were going, but there was even a rumour of Norway.

Then they heard the Germans were retreating so fast that they had left a hospital train in a siding, full of wounded men without food or water. It was days before they had been discovered so it seemed likely they would be nursing more and more of the enemy.

She suddenly cheered up. If they were moving that fast, the fighting couldn't be so intense, and it looked like it wouldn't last much longer, thank God.

For the first time in her letter that night, Lily wrote of her optimism that the worst was over, and she was looking forward *soon* to being his *bride*, his *wife*. Perhaps they ought to set a date for next year? There would be a lot of arrangements to be made.

She'd never written like that before — it always felt like it would be tempting fate.

And it was: there was one more horror that they *both* had to endure before they were to reach the broad sunlit uplands of Churchill's speech.

20

They had their supper together and Lily, thank God, seemed quiet, no aggression, just a vacant, far-off look.

Alzheimer's was such an awful disease, he thought, if for no other reason than in a happy marriage it ended the life of two people, not one.

Later, as the sun was setting, he announced his intention of taking a drive with her to see a friend from the past whom he'd met that day.

The nurse was startled, then tried to remonstrate with him, but he remained determined.

'It might do some good.'

He knew it wouldn't, but that didn't matter.

The nurse pointed out that he was too frail to manage on his own, but he brushed all criticism aside. She said she would ring the driver, she was sure he wouldn't mind driving him, but Mike had the keys for the car in his pocket where she couldn't get her hands on them.

He was adamant. Besides, he intended to

only be gone an hour at the most. Would she mind helping them to the car — and he needed his briefcase?

Still grumbling, she could see he was not going to give in, and he was after all her employer, so she helped reluctantly, fussing around Lily, getting her into her coat, even though, as he pointed out, it was a warm sunny evening.

'That's all very well, but your wife is vulnerable to chest infections, as you should know.'

He accepted the rebuke, knew it was true, and knew it didn't matter.

It took all of twenty minutes to get an acquiescent Lily into the car and belted up.

She looked around, giggling.

'Are we going for a drive?'

'Yes.' He nodded as he got behind the wheel.

She giggled again.

'Are you the chauffeur? What's your name?'

He winced. It still hurt. Deeply.

'Mike,' he replied.

Lily picked at something on her coat.

'That's a nice name. Where are we going?'

He went to kiss her on the cheek, but she shied away with a horrified look. Crushed, he remembered he was the chauffeur, not a husband. Another hurt — there had been so many over the last year.

He managed, 'Somewhere nice.'

He started the engine, put the automatic into drive, as the nurse said, 'Wait, you wanted your briefcase.'

He swore under his breath. He was so forgetful these days. What a mess that would have been.

'Yes — yes, thank you; it's on the bed in my room.'

The nurse came running back with it, opened the door and put it onto the rear seat.

He called 'Thank you' again as she closed the door.

Unhurriedly he carefully drove off, could see her looking after them in the mirror.

It wouldn't take much for her to call the police and start a manhunt to find them. He gave a grim chuckle. That was good to know.

★   ★   ★

They'd been in the Fatherland for over two weeks now. The sense, for the first time, of being the invader rather than the liberator was beginning to wear off. The Germans seemed just like anybody else.

To begin with the Tommies had been wary, even harsh. Coming across a row of dead civilians, including women and children, they found a local priest in a town was only blessing the Roman Catholics. The CO of one of the battalions drew his sidearm and threatened to blow the man's head off if he didn't bless them all.

Shaking, the priest did.

Another time, needing some boards to floor their treatment tent in a muddy field, he sent his men into a nearby farmhouse. They'd dragged out some heavy furniture and began to smash it up, the German wife wailing and crying as they did so. It made him feel rotten.

Now, at last, the master race was finally looking beaten. The soldiers of the Wehrmacht were beginning to surrender in their thousands, causing tremendous logistical problems.

On one of the first warm damp days of spring he sat on a purloined easy chair in the middle of a field and thought about the nature of war. There was no doubt about its evil and obscene nature — he could personally testify to that — but there *was* another side.

It was hard to explain as he looked around at his team, taking a rare moment of relaxation, kicking a football around, but there was a comradeship, a deep bond forged in all the fear and excitement of the past few months, that nobody in the civilian world would ever understand. And God, it seemed, had let him survive, to live a happy life with Lily.

Soon, they must surely be on their way home?

His moment of hopeful reverie was cut short by a corporal who came loping up, saluted, and handed him a message.

It was from the CO of the Guards battalion. Frowning, he opened it and read its contents. For a moment he couldn't understand why he was being told the startling news, then he read on.

Apparently the German Army had made contact with higher command, and negotiated a truce with an exclusion zone just north of their position.

It was to prevent the spread of typhus from some sort of camp called Bergen-Belsen, which was right in the middle of the line of advance. Allied planes were strafing the autobahns, and British troops were battling on the Lunenburg Heath right beside it. The fear was the epidemic could spread into both armies, and beyond.

Under the agreement, Hungarian and regular German Army troops would remain after the departure of most of the SS guards, to stop the inmates from fleeing into the countryside. After a week the guards were to be allowed to leave.

Next day, 15 April, the column got underway early. The CO had put him fourth in the line, right behind the lead tanks.

The countryside was beautiful, wooded hills and meadows with winding streams and pretty villages. And it was all so peaceful. Uncannily so.

Military policeman waved them on down a minor road.

They smelt it long before it came into view. The last time they had experienced anything like it was in Normandy, in the stinking fields of Falaise. Only this was worse — far worse.

The column rounded a wooded bend — and there it was.

The tanks stopped, but his jeep and two ambulances were waved forward to the open gates of the camp, the gates of hell on earth.

The shock of seeing German soldiers, still armed, standing alongside British sentries was soon obliterated from his memory as they drove into the camp and came to a halt.

Huge piles of emaciated corpses — little more than skeletons with a thin veil of translucent greenish flesh — were all over the area, and littered on the ground around them lay the living. He could hardly tell the difference, other than when an occasional skeletal arm was falteringly raised.

Some of the living lay with their heads against the rotting bodies of the dead. Flies, in their millions, rose in clouds into the air.

But the worst thing was an awful, ghostly procession, a silent host of diseased, still-living cadavers who drifted aimlessly around, with sunken eyes staring out of the deep sockets of the skulls.

He could see, literally, every bone in their bodies; there was no flesh, only the same, greenish translucent skin.

Their bellies were so sunken he could make out their spines from the front. Open, fly-covered sores were all over their bodies.

Despite the masks that they had donned, the stench was unbelievable.

Some of his men retched, vomited. He was informed by a colonel that there were approximately 55,000 still alive, with 10,000 dead, but the counting was still going on. Half-filled open pits full to the top with bodies were dotted around.

They were directed to one of the fifty poorly constructed wooden huts and told to deal with it. Inside, it had some bunks, but it was filled to overflowing with men in every state of emaciation and disease.

Later, he reckoned there were over 700 in the one hut. There were no lavatories or washbasins.

Locked in at night, the men had relieved and vacated themselves where they stood, between or on the people lying on the floor. They had sunk so low that there was no trace of humiliation or embarrassment. They had famine diarrhoea, passing nearly a dozen motions in the one day. The place was running in evil-smelling bowel fluid. Besides the typhus, dysentery was rife.

He didn't know where to begin. What filthy blankets there were, were teeming with lice — he could see movement in the material. Lice were instrumental in the spread of typhus.

He looked around at the shocked faces of his team.

'Right, let's get started.'

Gloved and masked, they began their work.

Once they had the poor souls outside, they were stripped and dusted with DDT powder and then given fresh blankets and transferred to newly erected tents. It took a week. The huts were then marked to be destroyed by fire.

Some of the SS guards who had been ordered to remain — men and women — were forced to collect the dead without gloves, risking catching typhus.

At one time shots were heard. A burial detail of Hungarians had refused to handle the dead bodies. A British officer, after twice warning the Hungarian captain, drew his sidearm and shot him dead. As the others tried to rush him, sentries opened fire with sten-guns. All were killed.

And it was discovered that SS guards were still shooting people in the vast camp, in an effort to cover up their actions.

They too were killed.

The women guards were made to live in one of the filthy huts and given the same basic rations as the prisoners and already some were showing signs of illness.

There was a rumour that two of the more sadistic male guards, who had been pointed out by the prisoners, had been thrown into one of the emptied huts, and had been kicked and punched to death by the enraged British troops. Along with the others the hut was set ablaze.

But there were other more upsetting incidents. Since their arrival at least another 2000 inmates had died — from being given food by the appalled troops. Their frail bodies had been unable to handle the richness and they had died in agony — of good intent.

Just under a hundred students in their final year at London teaching hospitals had been flown over, and Mike knew field hospitals were on the way.

Bulldozer tanks had dug huge pits, then shoved great tangled heaps of what once had been real people, with all their lives, loves and hopes now reduced to so much offal and bone, along the ground and into the yawning holes. The bulldozers began to refill the trenches with earth, covering the obscene sight, reversing over the soft earth with the odd arm still sticking out.

Emptied huts were being set ablaze by flame-throwers mounted on bren-gun carriers.

Mike took a last look around at the scene, as he was relieved and returned to front-line duty. As he stared at the flames, he knew he would never be able to view the world the same way again. You couldn't experience something like that and not be affected.

How could a loving God have allowed this to have happened? Some part of him, in his soul, had died. That men could do this to other men left him frightened.

Mike knew, and it shocked him, that there must be the potential for such evil in all of them.

The great palls of smoke rising into the air added an even greater feeling of doom, as if it were the end of humanity.

21

The war was coming to a close, everybody could see that. So when Matron called a meeting for six o'clock that night, it was eagerly anticipated that it might be news that they were going home.

The chatting stopped as Matron, in full regalia, the light reflecting off her major's crowns, strode in, flanked by a sister and a RAMC half-colonel.

They all stood up but were ordered to 'Stand easy — sit down.'

Matron looked around, seeming to examine every one of their faces personally before she spoke.

'We have with us Colonel Jones of the RAMC. He has come here today to ask for volunteers for a special job.'

There was complete silence.

Lily thought you could have heard a pin drop. What was coming?

'Our forces have liberated what can only be called Death Camps. There are literally thousands of patients who have been terribly ill-treated, and starved almost to the point of death. Dysentery and typhus are rife.'

They sat transfixed as she went on to describe what so far had been done.

'Now, we come to today. More help is urgently needed, particularly professional nursing skills. We are therefore being asked to do this work.

'However' — she looked around — 'I know you have seen suffering on a massive scale but because of the horrific circumstances — and they are truly unimaginable — this work will test you as nurses as never before, and because of epidemics of typhus, dysentery and cholera, we are asking on this occasion for volunteers.

'There will be no shame if you feel you are unable to undertake this work. You will be returned to the UK for posting to base hospitals. There is much to be done there.

'I will ask Colonel Jones to address you further, but first, can I have a show of hands from those of you who will volunteer for this duty?'

Not a single nurse failed to put up her hand.

Two days later they entered Belsen — Bergen in a convoy of ambulances. There was nothing that could have prepared them for what they saw.

Very little had changed. The inmates were continuing to die in their hundreds, the bulldozers were still at work, so were the flamethrowers.

Their duty was to tend to the women and children, to save as many as they could.

To begin with they salvaged two of the better huts, stripping them of the filthy straw and human waste and cleaning out the 'living' rags of clothing, making them into a bonfire. They then set about fumigating and scrubbing the floor with DDT and disinfectants.

Yet, afterwards, they were still aware of lice coming out of the cracks in the wood of the doors and walls, so the engineers gave them blow torches which they used whenever they found them.

Next, they tackled the women themselves, shaving off their filthy hair and putting them into big baths, cleaning the open sores which covered their bodies. They fed them specially prepared diets.

The women, who had been indifferent to the British soldiers — to them it was just another uniform — began to respond to the nurses, following them around, continually saying *Schwester* — Sister — over and over again, and kissing their hands.

German nurses had been brought in to work alongside them and, though efficient, they were terrified of catching typhus, with many going off sick.

Lily, for the first time ever, was unable to write to Mike. When she got back to her bed, in a tent outside the camp, her body ached all over, and she wondered for a moment if she was coming down with something. She needn't have worried: she was asleep in minutes.

The fact that she couldn't find the time to write made her feel guilty, although no letters had reached her for two weeks or more. But neither had they reached anybody else. It was obvious the chaotic times they were living through.

They were eventually able to move the women and children who had survived, to an old German Panzer barracks about a mile away. Here, they had proper beds, flowers, tables with tablecloths, pictures on the walls — and light, through big windows with trees beyond. Almost magically the women began to respond. Although deaths still occurred, the worst was over.

Though secretly there was originally great concern in the highest authorities that the nurses would break under the strain, they had responded magnificently.

The doctors had even made bets as to which one would crack first, but though they had become drawn, pale, with dark patches around their eyes, they had responded to the most dreadful conditions they would ever meet in their lives — and had prevailed. In order to keep going, they had even been given stimulant drugs.

All this was revealed by Colonel Jones who came to give them a farewell address, to thank them on behalf of the Allied powers for the sterling work they had undertaken. He finished with a broad smile, telling them that they were going to Denmark for a week's rest and relaxation.

Before they moved out Lily went for a walk in the beautiful countryside. Birds sang in the trees, water tumbled in the delightful little brooks that ran into lakes surrounded by wooded hills.

Heaven.

Yet less than a quarter of a mile away there had been a horror of unspeakable depravity.

Hell.

They had been wrong at Sunday school. Hell didn't have demons with forked tails and tridents: it had lice.

She sat on a log, got out her writing pad from her bag and began to pen the first letter to Mike in ages.

My darling
Forgive me for the lack of letters

recently, but we have been through a most difficult time.

I can't bring myself to tell you about it, but we have been in a place called Belsen, a Nazi death camp that the world will come to know for its pitiless barbarity.

Now it's over and we have been given a week's rest and a chance to relax, in Denmark. I do hope my letters will reach you.

The talk is, that after that we might all be going home, for good.

Mike, darling, I haven't heard from you now for well over two weeks, even a little longer. I do hope everything is all right with you. I have consoled myself with the thought that it's because we hear that the German defence has folded and that you are constantly on the move.

I pray to God that is so, and that very shortly it will all be over, and we can get on with our lives, in peace.

Well, darling, I'll finish now and get this off right away, as we are leaving within the hour.

I love you, need I say more? I'll say it again.

I love you.

Lily XX

But she was not to hear from him again during the war.

When it was over, it was a medical friend who managed to ring her in Denmark as they were celebrating the news of the German surrender, who told her about Mike. Lily, called to the receiver, listened, her face draining of all colour.

Immediately, without any authority, she left for Germany.

22

In the headlights the warehouse showed up starkly against the blackness of the night. He swung the car around the corner of the building, the beams picking up the back area. Several trailers, uncoupled, were parked in a row. As he drove on, the lights showed the ground beyond the tarmac that led down to the river's edge.

In a low gear he took the car over the boundary, bouncing on the rough ground until the engine stalled in the shallow ditch.

He looked at her sideways. The sleeping pill had worked ten minutes ago, when she'd suddenly gone quiet in the car. He'd managed to give it to her before the meal, unbeknown to the nurse. She was drowsy, eyes half closed, a smile playing around her mouth.

It was heartbreaking, a picture of Lily as she had been, the Lily he had loved for a lifetime.

★ ★ ★

Lily struggled to keep herself calm, looking out of the back of the lorry at the devastated city of Berlin, at a road running for miles between enormous mounds of rubble, and the stark outlines of still standing walls of bombed houses.

Hundreds of German women had been organized into gangs and were helping the army bulldozers clearing up. There were only very old and very young German men in sight.

The three-tonner let her off at the gates of an old *Wehrmacht* barracks.

She stood, clutching her brown case, looking in at the bleak, half-destroyed brick buildings, and the scores of newly erected wooden huts.

Redcaps were on duty at the barriers and a sign proclaimed British Military Hospital, known locally to the squaddies as the 'Lili Marlene' because there was a high wall still standing, and an old lamppost, looking remarkably like a scene on the sheet music cover for the song.

For a moment she stood under the lamppost willing herself to be strong, yet full of dread. Mike was in there and she prayed to God he was still alive.

Lily controlled herself, and marched forward briskly. A Redcap sergeant blocked her path, but she already had out her identity card.

After a fleeting look at it he stepped back and gave a crisp salute. 'Thank you, ma'am.'

Lily had on her best uniform, with skirt, her lieutenant's pips on her shoulders.

She returned her ID into her shoulder bag, and asked, 'Can you direct me to the ward for infectious diseases?'

He reached through the open window of the guardhouse and pulled out a clipboard, running the back of his finger down a list.

'Here we are — Block C, ma'am.'

He looked up and pointed.

'That's the hut over there, away from the rest, beyond the ambulances. You can't miss it, it's on its own.'

She thanked him and walked in its direction.

The Redcap watched her retreating shapely back and thought 'cracking bit of stuff'. Pity Block C was where they put the hopeless cases. Was she visiting, or reporting for duty? If it was for duty he might even try his luck. Although fraternizing with the commissioned nurses was forbidden, it happened all the time.

They even had invitation evenings between their messes.

Lily found the hut, as far from the main area as it was possible to get. At the double doors she hesitated, frightened of what she would find. She composed herself and went in. She was met by the sight of a nurse in full QA dress and veil, who looked up from her desk in surprise.

Lily introduced herself, all the time glancing beyond, down the row of beds, trying to see him.

'I'm Lily de Howarth, I believe you have a Lieutenant Gibson in your care. I would like to see him.'

The young nurse stood up, looked anxious.

'I'll get Sister — she's in her office.'

When she came, she was a tall woman in full red cape and grey dress and carrying three pips on her shoulders. She frowned at Lily.

'Can I help you?'

Lily steeled herself.

'I want to see Lieutenant Gibson.'

Sister shook her head.

'I'm afraid that's not possible. He has typhus and is not allowed visitors. There is a risk of infection. Anyway, may I know what is your connection with the lieutenant?'

Lily raised an eyebrow.

'He is my fiancé. I've just been nursing in Belsen. I take it you have heard of the place?'

Sister's face softened. 'I'm sorry I didn't know. That's where he caught it. Were you with him?'

Lily had only found out when her friend had phoned her. Before that she had had no idea.

'No. He was one of the first to liberate the camp.'

The woman weighed up the circumstances, and relented.

'Well, I shouldn't let anybody in but — follow me.'

Lily did, until she stood at the foot of his bed. It was all she could do to stop herself rushing forward, and to maintain her composure.

The Mike she knew was almost unrecognizable. His head had been shaved and his face was gaunt, eyes closed in sunken sockets.

Lily faltered. She knew near-death when she saw it.

'Is he naturally asleep?' she asked, but dreaded to hear what she suspected.

'No, my dear, he's sedated.'

Lily took a hesitant step nearer, but the sister put a hand on her arm.

'I think you ought to see Captain Lewis, he's the physician in charge.'

He turned out to be young, fresh-faced and straight out from home. But he knew his stuff. Apparently he'd been on a course at the School of Hygiene and Tropical Medicine, prior to posting to the Far East.

'So that's why they sent me to Germany.' He shook his head resignedly and pushed at the bridge of his glasses. 'Typical Army.'

Feeling frightened, and shivering a little with the shock of seeing Mike, Lily swallowed, and asked, 'Tell me please, the truth. What is the prognosis for him?'

Lewis glanced down at his patient's notes, read for a moment, and then looked up at her.

'You are an experienced nurse, so you don't need me to tell you it's not good. I'm sorry. Lieutenant Gibson has suffered the infection for some time, with constant delirium, sleeplessness, difficulty in swallowing, severe headaches — '

He looked away. 'Not very favourable.'

There was no doubting what he was implying.

There was silence in the room; the sound of birds in a tree outside made the silence inside even more intense.

She knew her face was wet. Lily found her handkerchief and dabbed at her eyes.

'I'm sorry.'

Lewis waited and said nothing.

She put her handkerchief away, and stared out of the window. Abruptly she turned back, and looked him in the eye.

'I want to nurse him.'

243

Lewis shifted his feet uneasily and began, 'I don't think that would be very wise, I mean — '

Lily cut him off.

'You just said it, I'm an experienced nurse. You can't afford the intense one-to-one nursing that I could give him.'

Lewis protested.

'What about your unit — they're not going to let you just leave them?'

Lily was adamant.

'I can swing that; leave it to me. Our hospital is on the verge of being disbanded and we're all being posted home. Anyway, I can take leave, they owe me a few weeks.'

Startled at her intensity, Lewis shrugged.

'I can't authorize anything, but if you feel so strongly, well, I'll see what I can do at this end.'

He didn't say what he was thinking, that it would be only for a week, maybe two at the most, because the patient would be no more.

He felt sorry for her; she'd been through a lot according to the sister. They all had. The QAs had more than earned the respect of every member of the army, right up to Monty himself.

He reached for the phone on his desk.

It was settled with startling swiftness. Mike's bed was put into an empty hut which was used for storing carbuoys of disinfectant and other containers.

A camp-bed for Lily was put alongside his.

Matron had been informed and came around immediately, eyebrows in a furrow of displeasure.

'I find this highly irregular, Nurse. If it wasn't for the captain's assessment of the case I could not possibly condone it.'

He'd told her of the expected outcome.

She sniffed. 'However, I have been informed that your service record is unblemished so, against my better judgement, I'm going along with it.

'You may use the mess for your meals and the service block for your ablutions, but, of course, you will not be taken on our strength, so there will be no service pay, at least not from us.'

Lily faced her.

'I understand completely, Matron. Now, I would like to get on with nursing Lieutenant Gibson.'

Matron had not been spoken to like that — ever. Speechless, she raised an eyebrow, took in the young, determined face before her. Perhaps it was because she knew she was Lieutenant the Honourable Lily de Howarth, perhaps it was because she respected her service record, but all she said quietly was,

'Yes — of course.'

When they were left alone at last, Lily leant down and kissed his clammy forehead, eyes welling up with tears as she stroked his temple.

'Mike, you're going to get through this, do you hear me? It's Lily, and I love you too much. You can't leave me. I won't let you.'

The next two weeks were a nightmare. He awoke rambling, shouting, arms thrashing about, swearing. Hot sweats, that left the bedclothes wringing wet, were followed by cold sweats, which did the same. Regular breathing broke frequently into laboured breathing. Heart-breakingly, at no time did he seem to recognize her.

Once, he reared up, swearing, grabbing her, eyes wild with terror, before collapsing back onto the bed.

Exhausted, she was asleep when he started moaning, clutching his head, moving it from side to side. His agony was dreadful to see.

On other days he saw visions of dead people, rising up out of the earth, reaching for him. Screaming, he backed up against the bars of the bed, swinging at them in terror, as she tried to calm him down. Because he couldn't swallow properly, her attempts to feed him ended usually in failure and he became progressively weaker.

In desperation, she persuaded Lewis to put new lines in, to keep him hydrated and fed, but he tore them out, sending blood everywhere.

Sedated again, he lay there as she looked down at his emaciated body — the once young, fit body that had given her so much pleasure, so much *love*.

When Lewis went she broke down, wept uncontrollably. He was losing the battle, and she knew it. When no more tears would come, Lily blew her nose and tidied herself up: there was work to be done.

She stripped off the bloodied sheets and remade the bed, rolling him gently from side to side as she did so. Then Lily gave him a bed bath, lovingly sponging and drying him like a mother with a young child.

She followed it with a shave; talking about nothing in particular as she lathered his face then carefully used a safety razor.

Finally, exhausted emotionally and physically, she lay on her camp-bed, staring up at the ceiling.

What would become of her if — ?

She couldn't let the thought grow — had to stop it right there and then — stop it, stop it, stop it.

Lily lapsed into an exhausted sleep, still struggling to keep the thought of his death out of her consciousness.

It was sunset when she awoke, long shadows of the trees outside stretching across the floor and up the wall. Light, coming through the leaves dappled the ceiling, little shadows moving from side to side. It was all so peaceful.

For several seconds she lay there, warm and contented, enjoying the peace.

The peace.

She frowned. It was never peaceful. If he wasn't thrashing about, his laboured breathing and coughing was ever present.

For a split second she was terrified, then snatched around and sat up —

His eyes were open, looking at her — properly looking at her.

Lily stared back.

Then, across the ravaged features, crept a slow smile. His cracked puffed lips moved.

'Hello, Lily.'

23

It took a while for him to be strong enough to be repatriated in a converted Halifax bomber back to Britain, accompanied by Lily.

When they touched down at Northolt the news had just come through. Japan had surrendered unexpectedly. Crowds were on the streets as they drove to the hotel in London she had arranged. As she checked them in, the place was heaving with celebrating people, kissing, drinking and dancing.

A battered white grand piano, showing its years of wartime misuse, was being played in the bar by a man in white tie and tails. He looked as if he had been up all night.

A woman in a black and silver cocktail dress was singing.

Just forget your troubles and learn to say
Tomorrow is a lovely day.

Lily couldn't help but think of all those poor boys who would never have a tomorrow, and all the thousands and thousands of others whose tomorrow had been blighted by terrible injury.

In their room, with the noise of the cheering crowds in the streets below, they just held onto each other, saying nothing.

It was, at last, all over.

When they drew apart, Lily looked up at him, searching his face.

'Promise me, you will never leave me again — ever. Not even for a day.'

His still ravaged features broke into a smile. 'I promise. And you?'

She nodded. 'I promise.'

★ ★ ★

Lily had missed the chance to stand for Parliament in the election that had seen Clement Atlee become the Labour Prime Minister with a landslide victory.

'Winnie', their great war leader, had been overwhelmed by a desire for change, that it would not be the same as after the last war, when the returning troops came home to find the promises made of a fairer England would be betrayed.

She realized that there would be no real chance of becoming an MP for another five years and, in any case, Mike was still so very weak, he would need her for some time before he was fully fit.

Whether his mother was scandalized or not

by their living together, Mike never really found out.

As soon as she could she came up on a bus to Victoria Coach Station to see her boy back from the war.

When they met she was dreadfully shocked by his appearance and burst into tears.

They took her for a cup of tea and reassured her that he was out of any danger and well on the way to a full recovery, although it would take some time. She said he looked like the pictures they'd seen of the liberated prisoners of the Japanese.

Afterwards, they took her back to their hotel where Lily had booked her in for a couple of nights.

There was no disguising the fact that they were sharing the same double room, but his terrible appearance, which had shocked her greatly, and the knowledge that the 'girl' had nursed him back from death's door, meant that she kept her thoughts to herself.

In the event, although she was initially awed by the fact that Lily's father was a lord, the women in his life got on very well together. Never before had Mike noticed how witty his mother could be.

When she went home, climbing up the steep steps of the coach, while the driver in his cab situated alongside the bonnet watched her, she was much happier than she had been on the journey up.

Almost as soon as she'd gone, Lily's parents had swept up to Town to see her, her father fitting it in with an attendance at the Lords.

Mike had been dreading it, had heard Lily on the phone to them saying, 'I'm not being headstrong, Mummy, I know exactly what I'm doing.'

They clearly thought that their daughter had gone off her head, slumming it by nursing somebody they had never met, had no knowledge of, and who was clearly not in the same social class. And she was living with him — that had come out somehow.

He wasn't disappointed. To begin with it *was* difficult.

Mike and Lily travelled to her parents' hotel, The Connaught, better she thought than their run-down hotel with its seedy implications.

In the lobby, as they stood waiting for them to come down the staircase, Mike found her hand.

She looked up at him.

'Don't worry, darling. You'll see, they are lovely people.'

He grunted. 'And I'm cohabiting with their *lovely* daughter, don't forget.'

Suddenly she squeezed his arm.

'Here they come.'

He watched in trepidation as the couple descended the staircase. Lord de Howarth turned out to be shorter than he expected, but well built, dressed in a country sports jacket, cavalry twills, and wearing brogues.

His wife was in a flowing chiffon dress of pre-war style, taller, a serene willowy beauty with eyes that had the same sparkle as Lily's, while her father had given her, albeit softer, his firm jaw-line and self-possessed manner.

Her father greeted her first, giving Lily a perfunctory kiss on both cheeks. As her mother said, 'Darling' and embraced her, Lord de Howarth turned to him.

He could not disguise his shock at Mike's appearance, as he said, 'So, this is the young man?'

Mike, still in his ill-fitting uniform, swallowed, and held out his hand.

'Yes, sir.'

Her father did take it, after an almost imperceptible pause — almost. His hand was strong, calloused. Lily had said he took an active part in running the estate.

Mike found steely hard eyes looking straight into his.

Lily turned from her mother, and took his arm protectively.

'Daddy, Mike has been very ill.'

She said it in a manner that warned her father he'd better be gentle, or else he'd have to deal with her.

'Have you now?'

Mike nodded. 'Yes, sir, and it was your daughter who saved my life.'

Lily gave a gentle tug on his arm.

'Don't be silly, darling, don't exaggerate.'

She looked at her father challengingly.

'Mike went through a lot in the war.'

Her father grunted. 'So did you, so did your brother, so did thousands of others.' He scowled, and added, 'And what about now? Surely he should be in a convalescent home? And to tell the truth, we're not happy about what you two are doing, it's immoral.'

Her mother snapped, 'Edward, don't be so direct.'

But her husband wouldn't be put off, and continued to look directly at Mike.

'We know nothing about you — your background — *nothing*, nothing at all. It's not good enough.'

Despite his weakness and a desire to get on with them, for Lily's sake and their future, Mike began to feel irritated.

'And I don't really know much about you — *sir*.'

There was a sharp intake of breath from

Lily and an awful silence.

It was broken when a slow grin spread across the rugged, weathered face of her father.

'My God, I wouldn't want to be around when you have a fight with my daughter — the two of you are a chip off the same block.'

'Daddy.'

But Lily was relieved.

And from then on the atmosphere lightened. Although her father continued to speak plainly he seemed less hostile.

Her mother looped her arm through Lily's free one and gently began to pull them both in the direction of the bar.

She knew her husband, and said lightly, 'Let's have a drink. It's wonderful to see you again, Lily. Come and tell us all about yourselves, what you have been up to. You must have seen some exciting things.'

Her father growled, 'Thank God that dreadful Mr Hitler's no more.'

As he took the lead towards the bar her mother exchanged a faint knowing smile with her daughter. Lily squeezed Mike's arm and whispered, 'Daddy will come round — he's a big softie really.'

They found a table. When the waiter came, her father automatically ordered two pink gins for the womenfolk — he seemed to know what they wanted — and a Scotch and water for himself.

'No damned ice like the Yanks, thank you very much.'

He turned to Mike. 'What will it be?'

Mike didn't know whether such a posh place as The Connaught served it or not, or how it would go down with Lord de Howarth, but, uncaring, he said straightaway, 'A pint of Guinness, please.'

Without batting an eyelid her father repeated it to the waiter, but added, half turning in his seat, 'Sure you wouldn't like a Scotch with that? Isn't that how you people take it?'

Mike flared. 'If you mean the real men who are the backbone of this country — the answer's no.'

There was a pointed silence and then her father's face broke into a sheepish grin.

'I asked for that. Bit upset about the daughter. I apologize.'

Relieved, Lily said, 'Daddy, I won't let Michael have spirits — his stomach isn't up to it yet. Guinness is the only drink allowed on the wards, you know.'

Her father chuckled. 'Sounds like she's nagging you already.'

Then he became serious and asked,

bluntly, 'So, when are you getting married?'

Mike looked at Lily for help as he said, guardedly, 'Well, we haven't set a date — '

Out of the blue, Lord de Howarth grunted, 'You're not a left-footer, are you?'

When Mike continued to look blank, he added, 'You know, a Roman Candlestick.'

It dawned on him what her father was driving at.

'No, sir, nominally C of E, but I'm not sure I'm even that now.'

Lily interrupted, looking from him to her mother.

'We are going to tie the knot in a Register Office, and we only want you, my brother and sisters, Mike's mother and a nursing friend there — Mike's not up to anything else.'

Her father glowered.

'Well, I don't really care what you are, or where you do it, but I don't like this living in sin.'

Her mother suddenly came to life, and said sharply, 'Edward, that's enough of *that*. You know damn well that you don't care a fig — what about all those friends of yours? You jolly well know their offspring are playing around — don't see you giving them the cold shoulder.'

Lord de Howarth looked wounded, and mumbled, 'That's because it's not my daughter, that's why.'

Lily's eyes flared like her mother's had.

'Stop it — both of you, and Daddy, I know it's because you love me, but don't worry, I know what I'm doing, and Mike's the man for me.'

Mike felt himself going red as she went on, 'We are getting married, that's all there is to it.'

Her father shot a nervous glance at his wife as he persisted.

'When?'

She looked at Mike anxiously.

'As soon as he is well enough.'

Lord de Howarth started to say, 'If he's well enough to — ' but stopped, not only because of the violent look in the eyes of the females in his family, but also he didn't know how to say politely what he meant.

As if to make amends he raised his glass in Mike's direction.

'Now that I've met you, I must say I find you better than I expected. You seem a decent enough young fellow, not on the make.'

Mike knew he wasn't being patronized, that his future father-in-law was just speaking his mind. He was just as truthful in his reply.

'Frankly, I was equally worried. I thought you might be some dim, chinless member of the aristocracy who had somehow produced a wonderful fiery daughter.'

He put his tongue in his cheek and carried on, 'Then I saw her mother and knew you'd married well.'

He didn't know where all that came from, and froze.

There was a second of silence in which the proverbial pin could have dropped, then her father roared with laughter, while her mother fluttered her eyelashes and giggled to Lily.

'You didn't tell me he was such a charmer, darling — and so observant.'

From then on, with the help of more drinks, a warmth came over the gathering, and by the time they'd had lunch — Mike having soup followed by cod cooked in milk — Lily was a happy woman.

They spent the rest of the afternoon back in her parents' suite, taking afternoon tea. Mike was impressed with the way her father could shovel slices of cake into himself after such an expansive meal.

All this, and the country was so drab. Austerity was the headline in all the papers and on the wireless, but money, as always, could insulate from hardship. Black market-eering was becoming a major problem.

On the way home, as they walked slowly through the London streets now just being lit by street-lamps that glowed dimly in the murky dusk, she squeezed his arm.

'Thank you, darling, you were wonderful.'

He stopped walking and turned her into him.

'They are very nice people. They love you dearly and must have had a terrible shock when you told them about me — I know I would have.

'If we have a daughter, I'll be just as protective.'

Her face, caught in the dim light coming from the converted Victorian gas-lamps, smiled up at him.

'Daughter, eh? How about a son?'

He kissed her softly on the lips, and whispered with his mouth still touching the corner of hers.

'We'll have two of everything, maybe three.'

She pulled away and smacked him on the arm.

'You'll be lucky.'

★   ★   ★

They were married at Westminster Register Office on 27 September 1945, he still in uniform as he would not be demobbed for a further four months. Afterwards the wedding party repaired to the Savoy for lunch.

He'd sent the money by postal order for his

mother to come up by train rather than the bus.

She'd insisted she didn't want to stay overnight, and he guessed that she might be worried and shy about meeting Lily's parents. In the event, to his relief and amazement, she acted with a calm assured composure and was laughing and joking with his, soon to be, in-laws.

He realized he'd only ever seen his mother at home, taking care of the meals, doing the laundry, holding down her various jobs. There had been no social occasions to observe her in another setting. Sadly, it might have been more obvious if his father had lived.

They said goodbye to her on the platform at Paddington, standing waving as the train pulled out. She leaned out of her open carriage window, waving back until it rounded a curve and she could no longer be seen.

Arm in arm, they walked back to the tube station. She knew he was exhausted, and asked anxiously, 'What would you like to do darling? Do you want to go home?'

'No, no.' He looked tired, but his eyes twinkled, as he said, 'It's the start of our honeymoon — how about a night at the pictures?'

Lily chuckled. 'You know how to treat a

new wife, don't you?'

They queued to see the new film *The Way to the Stars* with John Mills and Michael Redgrave.

That night, alone in the little two-bedroom flat they were renting in Bayswater, he took her in his arms.

'Mrs Gibson, thank you for marrying me, for becoming my wife.'

Her eyes flashed.

'And you, for becoming *my* husband, Dr Gibson.'

He grinned, and kissed her gently. Afterwards his face became serious.

'And thank you for saving my life.'

24

She straightened his tie and stepped back to look at him. He was dressed in his new double-breasted, pin-stripe demob suit.

It was ill-fitting, hanging loose from his still spare frame, and with his collar jutting out beneath his Adam's apple.

Anxiously he asked, 'How do I look?'

Lily smiled, and lied. 'Terrific.'

Then she thought it wasn't a lie really. Compared with what he had looked like even as little as a month ago, he was the epitome of good health.

He swallowed. 'Right, let's go.'

Outside, they boarded a bus going up West, and then changed to one bound for Tottenham Court Road.

Lily gazed out of the window, some of the anti-blast green matting still evident in the corners of the frame. In the weak sunshine she took in once again the awful threadbare and shabby look of Central London. Everywhere paint was peeling on doors and windows, and weed infested bombsites were everywhere. Eros was still boarded up, and now that the euphoria of the war's ending had passed, people looked worn out and under-nourished.

Rationing, far from being lifted, was getting even more severe. The danger, the community spirit, the determination to see the war through to the end, to win, had now evaporated. In its place was a bone-aching tiredness, both physically and mentally.

And on top of that thousands more men had yet to return to Civvy Street, including the prisoners-of-war they'd seen on newsreels from the Far East. The tales of their brutal, inhuman treatment had caused great anger in the country.

No, there was no continuing jubilation, but there was a Labour Government in power with a landslide majority of 145 and Clement Attlee as Prime Minister. The electorate had decided in the 'Khaki' election that, as Lily had predicted, Labour were better placed to deliver the rebuilding of a New Britain desired by so many.

She couldn't but wonder, had things been different, would she have been sitting in the House by then? But it didn't matter, was insignificant compared with Mike's health. Beside her, returned from the edge of death, was the one person in the world she loved above all else.

Now they were on their way to an interview

he was having at her old hospital, UCH.

He'd managed a sheepish grin when he'd told her *that*. The vacancy was in Casualty, a new post that was being created. She'd played along, joking they would never have *him* because of his King's background.

Secretly she prayed he would get the job; he was, after all, highly qualified after all his experience in the war. But then, so were many others, and she was frightened that they would take one look at him and reject him as not being fit enough.

They got off at the top of Tottenham Court Road near Warren Street Tube Station, and crossed the road, hand in hand, dodging between the buses and taxis.

When they reached the doors to the interview room they paused. Lily checked his appearance, picking some fluff off his lapel and using the back of her fingers to brush his shoulders.

'I look like a spiv in this suit.'

She continued brushing.

'Don't be silly, you look very professional.'

He grinned. 'My mother used to do this for me.'

She pulled a face, and said mockingly, 'Well somebody's got to look after you men, you are so helpless.'

On impulse he shot an arm around her

waist, pulled her to him and gave her a quick kiss.

'Mike.'

Holding her hat Lily looked around breathlessly, embarrassed at his behaviour, but the few people in the corridor didn't seem to have noticed.

His eyes were twinkling, in a way they hadn't for some time.

'I think I'm feeling better.'

Lily was delighted, but then her face clouded.

'Now, will you be all right? Do you want me to sit and wait with you?'

Aghast, Mike shook his head.

'Good lord, no. I don't suppose all the others will have their wives to hold their hands.'

Lily sniffed, knowing, of course, that he was right.

'Now, remember what I said — speak up and don't be afraid to ask questions.'

He nodded, more to satisfy her, then drew a deep breath and said, 'Right, here we go.'

It was her turn to suddenly go up on her toes and give him a peck on the cheek.

'I'll meet you in the Lyons Teashop on the corner then, after I've had a look around memory lane.'

He raised his eyebrows and pressed his lips together, nodded, took a deep breath and pushed through the double doors.

She had a glimpse of several men waiting nervously in obvious demob suits, then the doors closed off the scene.

Anxiously she turned away. It would be expecting a lot for him to get the job, yet she so wanted him to succeed.

Lily knew that he was very vulnerable at the moment, his illness, and what he'd been through, had left him weak *mentally* as well as physically.

Word was just beginning to circulate of the delayed effect on the sanity of some who had seen terrible things in the war.

When he'd first seen the advert in the *British Medical Journal* and said he might have a go, she'd tried to dissuade him, but he said he couldn't wait, as so many were coming home; he had to make a start as soon as possible.

Try as she might he persisted, and she had to admit he was only sitting around the flat, often in his dressing-gown until quite late in the day, sometimes very depressed.

Now, as she walked to the Nurses' Home, and with thoughts of also looking in on a couple of her old wards, her spirits sank. What was he going to be like when he came out? Would the disappointment set him back even further?

Lily found the hospital looking just the same, the Victorian and Edwardian brick buildings and white-tiled corridors and tunnels beneath the roads still there, albeit even older and more run down than before.

Some of the old, more inaccessible windows still had their criss-cross strips of brown sticky paper on them, put there to stop the glass flying in during bombing.

She met a few people who remembered her, and then bumped into Matron in her dark-blue uniform, white cap and silver clasped belt. The woman looked older and whether it was because she was to leave in the next six months, the war having delayed her retirement, but she suddenly beamed and said, 'de Howarth — isn't it?'

Lily said yes, but she was married now and was Mrs Gibson.

The woman who had terrorized all the student nurses said, 'Do come to my room and have a glass of sherry. You must tell me what you've been up to since you left here.'

When Lily got away, after recalling not the war, but memories of fire-watching drills, party invitations and the mischief that eighteen-year-olds away from home for the first time get up to, it was much later than she had intended.

Worried that he was already waiting for

her, and depressed, she scurried to the white-painted Lyons Teashop and went in.

It was busy, with the 'Nippies' as the waitresses were called, taking orders and going to the counter where other women were operating the chromium-plated boilers that provided the hot water for the tea.

There was no sign of him.

Relieved but puzzled, she settled into a chair, ordered tea and a rock bun for them both, and then watched the pavement outside.

She had sat in this same cafe as a student nurse, meeting others as they prepared for a night out 'up West' despite the war with its blackout and air raids. It was only a short while ago, yet after everything that had happened, it seemed another lifetime.

Ten minutes elapsed, and there was still no sign of him.

Lily began to think the worst — that he had fainted or something; he was still occasionally dizzy.

Then again, maybe he had been disappointed and couldn't face her, and was sitting on a bench somewhere.

To calm her nerves she opened her bag and took out her cigarette case, selected one, and lit up, breathing out the smoke just as the waitress appeared with a tray of cups, saucers, teapot and the plates with the rock cakes.

She nodded her thanks when it was all laid out, and poured herself a cup of tea, using the strainer.

Another ten minutes later and there was still no sign of him. Lily stubbed out the remains of the cigarette, finished her cup, and signalled to the waitress that she wanted the bill. She could wait no longer, determined to go looking for him, starting with where they had parted and, if she was told he had left, and she still couldn't see him, force herself to go into the two pubs in the area, even though, unaccompanied by a man, she would feel uncomfortable doing so.

Lily was just reaching for her coat, lifting it from the back of the chair and swinging it onto her shoulders, when she caught sight of his raincoated figure hurrying across the road.

Lily sank down, pushed her coat off her shoulders back onto the chair, and waited.

As soon as he drew near she tried to make out his face, but it was hidden by the brim of his trilby as he kept his head down. He was coming in through the door before she saw his face properly — and he saw her.

He grinned and waved.

Lily's heart leapt, he looked so happy.

As he reached her, she asked, 'Darling, are you all right, you've been so long?'

He slid into the chair opposite, removing his hat.

'Yes — sorry. I was talking — very interesting.'

Lily was delighted. 'Talking — you got the job then?'

Mike shook his head.

'Oh no, they said it was going to one of their own chaps; he's just been released from the air force — early, apparently. He was in post when he was called up.'

'Oh.' She was bitterly disappointed. 'That's unfair, why did they advertise then?'

He shrugged. 'It was already too late to stop the process, and in any case . . . ' He grinned.

Puzzled, and a little annoyed, Lily frowned.

'So what have you been talking about, and to whom?'

Mike's eyes were more alive than she had seen them in a long time. He nodded at her handbag.

'Can I cadge a fag?'

Lily was pleased and irritated at the same time. She found her case again and he took one, and held it in the flame of her lighter before she did the same to her own — Lily felt she needed it.

She leant back, blew out the smoke.

'Well?'

Annoyingly he nodded at the teapot.

'You going to be Mother? I could murder a cup of tea.'

'Oh, Mike, stop teasing. Why are you so happy?'

He relented. 'Well, you know all this talk about the Labour Government bringing in a National Health Service next year?'

She snorted. 'Of course I do, silly, what about it?'

Enthusiastically, Mike explained.

'In anticipation, UCH are preparing to expand some of their departments, and one of them is Radiology. They expect there will be a great increase in the demand for X-rays, and they are understaffed as it is.'

She frowned. 'How did this come up?'

Mike shrugged. 'We were all invited to stay after the interview, they had one or two other propositions and thought it a good time to air them while we were there.'

Lily looked at him in disappointment.

'But, darling, radiology? It's not an area you've had real experience, and besides . . . '

When she paused, he asked, 'What?'

'Well, after the sort of work you have been doing I thought general surgery was the aim. You have a real talent and, sadly, wonderful experience — and with great praise I might add.'

Troubled, he looked away.

She waited, suddenly aware that he was struggling to say something.

Eventually he faced her.

'To tell you the truth, Lily, I don't want to be involved in that kind of thing anymore: I've seen enough.'

Lily looked at him, searched his face.

'You poor thing, I had no idea . . . '

He averted his eyes, staring into his teacup.

'I didn't know how to bring it up before; in fact, at one point, I was on the verge of giving up medicine altogether.'

Apologetically, he added, 'I tried for the job to see if I would get over it — and, besides, I owe it to you.'

Lily reached out, put her hand over his.

'Oh, darling, you owe me nothing. Anyway, how do you mean *owe* me?'

Mike pulled his chin into his chest in a gesture of the obviousness of what he was about to say.

'You're my wife. We've got a life to live, children to bring up. It's up to me to look after you.'

There was no way Lily would hurt his feelings, but the fact that she had enough money to support them was, she knew instinctively, not the thing to say, not to any man worth his salt.

But she could not stop herself saying, 'Mike, you know I don't intend to be just a wife and mother, don't you?'

He frowned. 'Yes, of course, but that's not the point.'

She let it pass, picked up the teapot and played 'Mother', putting the strainer over his cup and pouring more tea.

'So, radiology. What's the attraction?'

Mike shrugged. 'It's one step removed, isn't it, from all the pain and grief of dealing with the patient and their families?' He gave a humourless chuckle. 'It was either that or pathology.'

She digested this fact, and frowned.

'But don't you have to be good at maths or something? They always look as if they are doing calculations.'

His face lit up. 'Well, that's what did it for me. I was very good at physics for my matriculation. It seems I was streets ahead of the others answering a couple of calculations they threw at us.'

He was full of eagerness as he told her what had happened, then eventually he calmed down.

'It will be six months on a very low salary.' Guiltily, he continued, 'It will be difficult . . . '

Lily had seen the enthusiasm, the new life

in his eyes as he had explained and, although she was disappointed by the outcome, it could have been, as she had feared, a flat rejection.

The fear of his appearance came back to her. Despite it, they had wanted him. She couldn't complain.

'We'll manage and, in any case, I've got some news for you.'

He looked up sharply. 'What, since I've been on the interview?'

Lily confessed, because she had to.

'No, of course not. I was going to tell you before, but I didn't want you distracted in any way.'

'Well?'

Lily became uncharacteristically reticent.

'I've had an offer.'

He prompted, 'Of what?'

She finally came clean.

'There has been the death of an MP — in a constituency near home. It was Conservative held, mostly county but with an area of a large town — the boundary has been redrawn. I've been invited to a selection interview. They seem to think that I might have a better chance than a man in a flat cap — and we are well known in the district.'

She giggled nervously.

Actually, she'd had the offer for over a

week but had been too frightened of upsetting things just as he was bracing himself for the interview, and worrying about getting his life back on track.

'So what are you saying?'

Cautiously, Lily began, 'We can manage, because for the next month, at least, I will be away a lot of the time, getting fed and watered by the party so it won't cost us very much.'

She didn't say that, despite her politics, her father had agreed to give her a generous allowance to cover expenses, because secretly he was very proud of her.

'After that, who knows? If I get in . . . '

For a moment Mike was stunned, didn't know what to say.

In the silence, Lily begged, 'Please, Mike, you know how much it means to me — but I won't do it without your support.'

Gently he accused, 'And you never said anything.'

Lily hung her head.

'I didn't want you bothered just before the interview. I would have got around to it eventually, of course.'

It was not like Lily, but she waited in trepidation, conscious of the shock it must have been. Inwardly she prayed that he would be understanding. She craved his blessing, knew, that despite everything, she would not go ahead without his approval because she loved him like no other. In that respect, she was already different from the Lily before Michael Gibson.

The silence seemed to last forever. Then he finally spoke.

'Of course, you *must*.'

'Oh, Mike.'

She forgot all decorum, jumped out of her chair and gave him a great big hug, much to the startled, tired-looking Londoners around her.

Except for one old lady in the corner.

'For Gawd's sake be careful, luv. Looks like you could kill him.'

25

'Thank you for saving my life.' His words echoed in his head from down the years. And now, this was the way he was going to repay her? But she would wish it too. Perhaps, in that tormented brain she was willing him on.

They had sworn never to be parted. Despite their busy careers they had always spoken daily, even, if necessary, by the telephone shared with three other households on the same line.

But this disease had parted them as surely as death.

More than death.

Wearily, he got out of the car leaving the headlights on, and stumbled to the river-bank. He spread out a rug and a few things he had brought in his briefcase, then went around to her side and opened the door.

Lily jerked awake as he started to try and get her out and began to fight him off.

Eventually she stood up, hanging onto the open door, her face caught in the reflected light from the headlamps. Her eyes flared.

'What's this, what are we doing here? Who are you?'

He pretended to smile.

'It's a party. You like parties, don't you, Lily?'

'A party — out here?'

'Yes, come on.'

He held onto her as they staggered over the rough ground. He pointed to the rug.

'Look, let's sit here, there are drinks and things to eat. Take your coat off.'

Her mood instantly changed and she giggled.

'What fun.'

She pulled away from him and went to the rug, settling down slowly and reaching for one of her favourite snacks — marshmallows.

He stood, looking down at her, the lump in his throat causing him so much pain he couldn't speak for a while.

★ ★ ★

Lily won with a majority of 104 after two recounts.

In the next month, as she was welcomed into the Commons, and schooled in its ways and traditions and was listened to politely and without interruption, as was the custom with maiden speeches, Mike presented himself to the new department and began the course in radiology.

As the year of 1946 drew to a close, they were still living in Bayswater, but hardly seeing each other as Lily continued to attend the House and went down to the constituency most weekends, whilst Mike worked all sorts of shifts and attended courses.

On a very cold New Year's Eve they went to see Ivor Novello's show *Perchance to Dream* at the Hippodrome, and then dinner for two at The Dorchester, the treat on her, which he graciously accepted with a grin.

'It's time you kept me in the manner I am beginning to be accustomed to with all these House of Commons junkets on the Terrace.'

She clinked her champagne glass against his; glad to see he was relaxing despite missing each other. He had been working very hard and was due to take his exam soon. As she looked at him across the candlelit table she saw a fit Mike, filling out his evening jacket, the stiff, winged collar of his shirt and white tie hard against his neck. There was no trace of his previous fragility.

Lily chuckled. 'That's a change of heart, isn't it?'

He smiled. 'I don't mind living off your immoral earnings as a Labour MP.'

She frowned. 'Mike, that's not fair. I work jolly hard for a fairer society. You of all people should understand that.'

'You mean, from my sort of background?'

Lily said, 'Yes' and instantly regretted it, then was irritated by the fact.

'Mike, why are you so anti my party?'

'Well, they're making a mess of the Health Bill for a start — ' Her stony face made him stop, smile, and say semi-jokingly, 'And because they see more of you than I do.'

That, she knew, was true.

'I'm sorry, but you knew what I was like when we met. I never hid it from you.'

He angled his head, nodded in acknowledgment, but said, 'Remember, we swore never to be parted — ever.'

Lily winced. 'I know, but it's life. Anyway, we talk every day, and when you've finished training perhaps you could get a post in or near the constituency.'

He snorted. 'What good will that do? During the Parliamentary session you will be up in Town.'

There was no answer to that.

Mike changed the subject. He had no desire to spoil the evening, and besides they were the lucky ones. All over Britain there were wives missing husbands, or coping with the mental and physical aftermath of the trauma of war. They had come through unscathed — just about — and both had good jobs.

Millions of men had come home to terraced houses with outside lavatories and no washing facilities other than the galvanized bath hanging outside the scullery wall.

In the tenements it was even worse. He often wondered why he wasn't a socialist like, ironically, his upper-class wife; why he was sceptical about the new Health Service to be, that Bevan was guiding through its stages in Parliament?

Though it was undoubtedly born from a Christian desire to make a better life for people, like his mother for instance, colleagues worried about the 'bottomless pit' of money that it would require, and that with the Welfare State they would be creating a society that was less self-reliant, more dependent on the state for everything. And, he realized, he was inclined to agree.

But he dismissed saying anything, avoiding getting into an argument. It wasn't appropriate tonight of all nights, so said, cheerfully, 'Anyway, as long as you continue to phone every day we are apart, that will have to do for now.'

Relieved, she smiled back at him over the rim of her glass.

'I promise — and you do the same.'

'I promise.'

At midnight, as the chimes of Big Ben rang

out over a radio, the 'Old Year' with a white beard and dressed in a long white gown with a notice pinned to it proclaiming '1946', passed through the ballroom, followed by a scantily clad young lady in a short white toga carrying a notice with '1947 Happy New Year'.

A piper, in the full uniform and regalia of the Scots Guards led her between the tables.

They touched their glasses charged with fresh champagne as he said, 'Happy New Year, darling.'

Lily responded, 'Happy New Year, Michael.'

They got up and joined everybody holding hands and singing 'Auld Lang Syne', rushing into the middle with ever increasing boisterousness.

Afterwards they danced for another hour, taking part in a conga that snaked out of the hotel past hooting taxis and throngs of people on Park Lane and then back into the hotel again.

With their champagne bottle empty, they left, holding hands as they walked through the streets and parks, all the way home.

She led the way into the flat, switching on the light.

'I still want to rush and close the curtains.'

She made for the little kitchen, and called over her shoulder, 'Would you like a Horlicks, or tea, or even that wretched Camp coffee you drink so much of?'

But before she could reach the kitchen, discarding her fox fur on the back of a chair on the way, he caught up with her, spun her round and kissed her long and passionately. Her black, close-fitting dress that she had saved up her clothing coupons for, and had bought in Swan & Edgar in Piccadilly Circus, was unbuttoned and fell to the floor.

Lily was in her petticoat when he lifted her up, carried her to the bedroom and lowered her onto the bed.

It all happened so swiftly; both were taken with the moment.

She hung onto him as he drove into her in a frenzy, one arm around her back, hard on her shoulder, the other clamped on her thigh, over her suspender. When he was spent he fell exhausted onto the bed beside her.

Lily made no attempt to rearrange her underwear, just lay there, wide eyed.

Eventually she propped her head on her hand, and looked at him.

'Phew, what got into you?'

He reached out, and ran the back of a finger lightly on her cheek.

'I don't know, the sight of your rear, I suppose.'

She gave him a playful smack on his naked

hairy leg, above his trousers, which were around his knees.

'That was very naughty, but as your Member of Parliament, I would like to thank you for your donation.'

With that they fell giggling into each other's arms again.

It was while he was caressing her silk-covered belly that she suddenly tensed.

'Oh, my God, Mike, you didn't use protection.'

He pulled a face, and apologized.

'Sorry, I wasn't thinking — must have been the drink.'

He tried to reassure her, not very convincingly, that she was unlikely to have conceived.

Mike was soon deeply asleep, but Lily remained wide awake, staring worriedly at the ceiling. She was one of only a handful of females in the House, some twenty-four in total for all parties, and she knew that most of her male colleagues on both sides of the political divide were still pretty dismissive of women in politics.

God forbid she became pregnant.

★ ★ ★

On 4 October, Lily gave birth to a 6lb 5oz baby boy at the North Wing of Bedford

General Hospital. Her husband was in attendance, one of the new radiologists on staff.

They had a house now, a modest Edwardian building ten minutes' walk from the station, which she used to get to her nearby constituency, and on to London.

Mike was now the proud owner of a pre-war Rover 12.

After the awful shock of finding herself pregnant, Lily had carried on working right up to the last minute, and only took two weeks off before she reappeared, briefly, in the House.

Even then, she had already been working on her correspondence from home.

It was unusual to say the least for a woman in public life not to withdraw under such circumstances, so she had carefully chosen ill-fitting clothing, and didn't show until the last few weeks.

There were still some shocked looks, and she was aware of whispering behind her back, and comments and snide little pieces in the gossip columns of Fleet Street.

There was even an attempt by the local party to de-select her.

But she had survived, and one of the nicest things to happen to her came from an unexpected quarter.

Lily was stopped in the corridor by none other than Winston Churchill, and congratulated in his rich unmistakable voice on her safe delivery.

She noticed, however, that he looked much older, more tired than he had ever looked during the dark days of the war less than three years ago.

The boy was christened James, after Mike's father, in the Chapel of St Mary Undercroft in the crypt of the Palace of Westminster. Mike's dear mother, though still remarkably composed, could not believe what was happening as she stood, surrounded by people she only saw photos of in the papers, and heard on the wireless.

Afterwards, they had a reception on the Terrace as tall-funnelled tugs, pouring black smoke towed rows of barges up and down the Thames, to and from the Port of London.

The following year Julia arrived, and Mike changed the Rover for a shiny new black and maroon Riley 2.5 with its long flowing mudguards.

His mother lived long enough to know that Lily was pregnant again, but never saw Alexis.

In the General Election of 1950 Lily was one of the sitting Labour MPs to buck the trend and be re-elected, although by this time Labour were down to a majority of only five.

By now she was having grave doubts about Socialism, and the Brave New World it was creating.

Quietly she resolved not to stand for re-election at the next Parliament, and with such a small majority the government was short lived.

Lily accepted several unpaid directorships on charities and was to receive the OBE in the New Year's Honours List of 1959.

The years passed, and James, Julia and Alexis graduated from law and medical schools and eventually married after some heartaches, their father grumbling about the expense.

Lily's parents moved to Australia to offset her mother's increasing arthritis, but when her father died some years later, she came home to live with them.

In the fifties and early sixties, girls and youths became teenagers, at least in Britain, then along came the Beatles, the IRA outrages, the start of organ transplants, and the relentless rise of women in all walks of life — and the collapse of the old social mores.

People lived openly out of wedlock — Mike smiled at the memory of his father-in-law's outrage — and the word gay was used for homosexuals.

The world had changed, and was continuing to change, and they both tried to keep a balanced opinion, knowing that it was easy to see their youth through rose-tinted spectacles, but, the war aside, they viewed the past, with its manners, the cheerful decency, the enforced lack of materialism, as something good that had been lost, perhaps for ever.

And Lily had to admit that though she considered great social advances had been made in the early days, the culture of benefits and the rampant trade unions of the 70s had mostly been her party's fault, particularly the reduction in grammar schools, which had served the poor so well.

Michael, meanwhile, had become well known in radiological circles, and worked with others in London and Cambridge on developing new equipment and diagnostic techniques.

To his astonishment, near the end of his career, he was approached by the Honours Committee and offered a knighthood.

Lily was overjoyed.

'At last you can get that chip off your shoulder about my being the Honourable.'

Even in his advancing years, he was still very fit, thanks to golf and gardening, and he chased the 'Honourable' around the drawing-room trying to smack her still pert derrière.

Over a bottle of wine she agreed he'd never had a chip, and he agreed to accept the honour.

Lily was so proud of him at the investiture at Buckingham Palace, decked out in his morning suit, once dark hair now grey, showing at the sides of his top hat as he posed for a photograph holding the award.

Afterwards, accompanied by the whole family they dined at Claridges.

It was the end of a marvellous year in which James had been made one of the youngest judges in the country.

The first sign of problems had come two years later, years of travelling the world, of seeing grandchildren start to mature, and prepare to attend college and university.

Lily had gone into town one day, shopping, and had been found by a policeman, vacant and troubled.

From her purse he'd established her home address and telephone number.

Mike, who had been in the garden, straightaway drove into town and went to the police station.

Her eyes had lit up with relief on seeing him, and she immediately remembered where she had left her car. With apologies to all she had driven home, closely followed by Mike.

An anxious week passed in which he had

watched her like a hawk.

Just when it seemed it was one of those aberrations that sometimes occurred in the complex wonderful organ that is the human brain, it happened again, only this time right in the middle of a shop — and he was only a short distance away.

After that he remembered all the little moments of increasing forgetfulness that they had put down to their increasing years.

Tests and scans, ironically some of which he had worked on in their development, were started, and at last a diagnosis was made: *Alzheimer's.*

At first Lily had shrugged it off with her usual, brisk aplomb.

But later, he had found her crying in the conservatory.

'Oh, Mike, I'm so frightened. What's going to happen to me?'

He had taken her in his arms, kissed the top of her head, and stroked her hair.

'Darling, I'm here. We'll all just carry on as usual. Don't you worry about anything.'

But worry *he* did.

He'd had one scare, being diagnosed with cancer. Carstairs had handled his treatment, and they seemed to have got on top of it.

So he'd agonized over many things, the most important of which was, what would happen to Lily if he died first?

There was enough money for a nursing home and the children would ensure everything was all right, although they had families and full lives to live.

But she would be in the hands of strangers, however well intentioned and good they were. Even though he would be dead, it would be as if he had abandoned her — Lily, the love of his life. It was unthinkable.

His cancer fortunately remained in remission, and Lily's condition, with medication, stabilized for some time, but suddenly, over one weekend, it became worse.

The more it took away Lily's dignity, the more pain it gave him, until that first day when she had woken up and didn't recognize him, and his heart broke.

Three months later his cancer returned with a vengeance.

26

Painfully, because of arthritis, he settled himself alongside her on the rug.

Lily paused from eating to frown at him.

'Who did you say you were?'

He sighed. 'I'm Mike.'

She looked around. 'Where are the others?'

'They'll be here in a minute.'

He poured out two gins, added angostura bitters and into hers, something else. She still had the taste for a pink gin.

He held out a glass.

'Here, have a drink.'

She took the glass and gulped down a third of it.

Mike tensed. He had started the beginning of the end. The end of a story of love.

'Why are you crying?'

She was staring at him; glass in one hand, chocolate éclair in the other.

'Something in my eye.'

She lost interest as soon as she said it, and returned to her eating and drinking.

Mike took a sip, gulping loudly as it went over his swollen throat.

He was killing the one person he loved

most in the world, who had nursed him back from the brink of his own death.

Unaware, Lily finished her gin. When she lowered her glass her eyes found his. Immediately they hardened.

'What are you looking at?'

'Sorry.' He looked away. 'Would you like another one?'

Lily paused, couldn't seem to make up her mind, swayed a little, then silently she held out her glass.

He poured in some more gin, added the bitters.

'Do you want another marshmallow?'

Lily shook her head, which began to drop. He watched as her chin slowly reached her chest, stayed there for a while, and then jerked back up, only for the whole process to start again.

Mike reached out, took the glass from her hand.

As she began to slip sideways he caught her, and laid her gently down on the rug.

The moment had come.

He put everything out of his mind and went through the routine, just as if he was treating a patient.

Everything was prepared.

From his briefcase he took the syringe and Velcro tape, pushed up her sleeve, applied the tourniquet and rubbed the skin in the hollow of her arm until the veins showed.

Pulling her arm straight he thumbed off the cover then pushed the needle into her, releasing the tourniquet.

It took four seconds, before he withdrew.

Sobbing, he buried his head in his hands. After he had composed himself, he leaned over her and their lips touched. Their last kiss on this earth.

What happened next, was a miracle: her eyes suddenly flew open.

'Mike.'

There was no mistaking the soft knowing look of love.

Then they closed — never to open again.

Mike stumbled back, stood trembling for a long time as he gazed down at her.

She looked serene, peaceful, her face like of old, devoid of the anger and frustration of the last few months.

Slowly he took off his jacket, tossed it aside, and sat down beside her, reaching for her hand.

She was still warm — was still Lily.

Once the biochemistry of life ceased, and a body was cold, that was different. There was nothing left, only a husk where once there had been a human being. Some believed it was because the soul, the spirit, had flown.

He didn't know, but after the war — and Belsen — he'd never been able to believe in a God who intervened in the lives of His people.

But love — what was that all about? How could you explain love?

He rolled up his sleeve, tightened the tourniquet around his left arm, and bunched his fist several times. He aimed at the hollow of his arm, then plunged the needle into his vein, drawing back to make sure he was in, then released the tourniquet.

He threw it away, and the syringe when he'd finished. Shaking, he lay down beside her and found her hand again. It was cool now, like it might have been on a winter's day.

Squeezing it, he whispered, 'Together again — for keeps.'

He waited.

Waited.

Strangely, it seemed to be getting lighter and, as he lay there, he was aware that the noise from passing high-speed trains on the new line was gone; he knew without turning his head, that the warehouse was no longer there, that the rubbish in the stream and on the ground had disappeared.

And it was warm, beautifully warm, and the sky was bright.

Something made him turn.

And there she was, Lily, with her laughing blue eyes and blonde hair, just like it had been, just like it always would be.

★ ★ ★

Lieutenant Douhet of the Police Nationale stared down at the two old folk lying hand in hand.

The doctor had given the time of death as somewhere between 9pm and midnight. Given the rug, the discarded syringes and tourniquets and a bottle of gin, a suicide pact seemed to be the most obvious scenario.

He drew on his Gauloise, and checked the time on his wrist-watch.

The police cameraman, with one last photo taken directly above them, called out that he'd finished his work, so Douhet nodded at the waiting forensic team and the medical examiners to carry on.

They moved forward, and brushed aside the plastic bags and other bits of rubbish that had lodged against the bodies in the morning breeze, and started to lay out their black canvas bags with zips.

Douhet watched, and then, finishing his cigarette, flicked the butt into the river where it died with a hiss.

He shook his head in disbelief. Funny place

to commit suicide, in a dump like this. With a roar another train passed by.

Still, his police career of nearly thirty years had taught him that the ways of mankind were not for a mere mortal to pretend to understand.

He hurried away, taking out his mobile phone.

His daughter was marrying later in the day, and he had been unexpectedly called to this scene, and knew he was going to be in trouble with his wife.

So he didn't see that it took the medical attendants quite some time to separate the entwined hands.

Other titles published by
The House of Ulverscroft:

THE TEARS OF AUTUMN

David Wiltshire

It is 1938. For two couples honeymooning in Sorrento, the future is uncertain. When Biff and Rosemary Banks meet Konrad and Anna von Riegner they become friends. Biff is a pilot in the RAF and Konrad an Oberleutnant-zur-See in the German Kriegsmarine. Together they tour the Amalfi coast, and visit the ruins at Pompeii. As they part, swearing undying friendship, they resolve to meet again in a year's time. Yet eleven months later their countries and their friendship are torn apart by a war that lasts for six years. At the end of it, will their friendship have survived?

OVER HIS DEAD BODY

Laurie Brown

Ever since Caroline Tucker moved back home from Hollywood to the bright lights of Haven, New Mexico, she's been trying (and failing) to avoid her ex-husband, town sheriff Travis Beaumont. However, she's forced to call him when her niece stumbles across the perfectly preserved body of a cowboy at Girl Scout camp. But is this a crime scene? Or is it just a potential tourist attraction? The mystery of the mummy unravels and Travis digs up some sinister evidence. And the more Caroline tries to keep away from trouble — and Travis — the more they come knocking at her door . . .

ALWAYS THE BRIDE

Jessica Fox

Nobody gets it right all the time. But Zoe Forster always strives for perfection. So when the fortune-teller at her hen party predicts she will marry twice, she's seriously unimpressed. Everyone knows Zoe and Steve are meant to be together. Still, even a marriage made in heaven has to survive in the real world and, a year in, things are getting predictable. Then super-sexy movie star Luke Scottman makes a repeat appearance in Zoe's life, and Zoe and Steve make some unwelcome discoveries about each other's less-than-perfect pasts. It seems the fortune-teller's prediction is about to come true after all . . .